After the **WRECK**,
I Picked Myself UP,
Spread My WINGS,
and **FLEW AWAY**

After the WRECK, I Picked Myself UP, Spread My WINGS, and FLEW AWAY

Joyce Carol Oates

Harper Tempest
An Imprint of HarperCollinsPublishers

HarperTempest is an imprint of
HarperCollins Publishers.

After the Wreck, I Picked Myself Up, Spread My Wings, and Flew Away
Library of Congress Cataloging-in-Publication Data

Oates, Joyce Carol, date

After the wreck, I picked myself up, spread my wings, and flew away / Joyce Carol
Oates. — 1st ed.

p.   cm.

Summary: Blaming herself for the car accident on the Tappan Zee Bridge that
killed her mother, fifteen-year-old Jenna undergoes a difficult physical and emotional
recovery.

ISBN-10: 0-06-073525-2 (trade bdg.) — ISBN-13: 978-0-06-073525-8 (trade bdg.)
ISBN-10: 0-06-073526-0 (lib. bdg.) — ISBN-13: 978-0-06-073526-5 (lib. bdg.)

[1. Loss (Psychology)—Fiction.   2. Death—Fiction.   3. Emotional problems—
Fiction. 4. Drug abuse—Fiction. 5. Traffic accidents—Fiction.] I. Title.

PZ7.O1056Af 2006

[Fic]—dc22   2005029059

                                                              CIP

                                                              AC

Typography by Joel Tippie

1 2 3 4 5 6 7 8 9 10

❖

First Edition

For Gloria Whelan

After the **WRECK**,
I Picked Myself UP,
    Spread My WINGS,
and **FLEW AWAY**

Prologue

Went off somewhere and when I came back Mom was gone.

It wasn't my fault. Don't blame *me*.

We were crossing the Tappan Zee Bridge headed west. The sun in our eyes. The sun was this mad red eye inside a bank of sick-looking clouds. The sun was blinding, glaring off the car hood. Mom's car on the Tappan Zee high above the Hudson River where you can feel the wind shaking the car even on days when there isn't much wind on land, and I'm sliding a CD in and the mechanism rejects it which happens sometimes and is so damn annoying so I push "CD" again and this time the CD stays in and I'm shading my eyes against the glaring sun and suddenly I am seeing a baby deer in the lane just ahead!—or maybe a dog!—this shadow shape Mom doesn't seem to see and I'm panicked screaming *Mom! Watch out!* and (maybe) I am grabbing at the wheel or (maybe) I am trying to grab at the wheel or (maybe) Mom is the one to turn the wheel (maybe) because I am screaming or (maybe) did Mom see the baby deer or the dog or (maybe) it was a large bird like a hawk, a goose . . .

And the car sprouts wings and *flies*.

It did! Yes, it did.

I

In the Blue

1

In the blue we were snow geese flying.

These big beautiful white-feathered snow geese flying with a flock of other geese. In the V formation we were flying and our long necks were sticking way out and our eyes were narrow slits in our weird white feather faces. And our wings!

You should have seen our wings pumping the air. Pumping the air, riding the wind.

A thousand feet above the river, pumping the air hard to save our lives.

A song came into my head.

> *Knew this old world would be a hard hard place*
> *Seeing how the snow geese fly, brave wings pumping*

2

It was a Time of Forgetting.

In the blue it was a long time, wish wish wish it would never end.

You sleep a lot. You dream but don't need to remember.

Like clicking through 101 TV channels on "mute." By the time you click through them all and return to 1, you don't remember a single thing you saw, so you click through them all again.

Or not. Kick the remote off the edge of the bed.

Lots of songs flew into my head in that time. Out of the sky these songs would fly into my head. Afterward I would forget them all. Except one.

In the Country of the Blue

there is no you

3

. . . so happy, she was saying *Of course I love you Jenna, my little lovebug Jenna. And I forgive you.*

All the ages I'd ever been. *In the blue* you can choose. I was four years old and my hair was a fluffy pale blond not this darkish dirty blond and Mommy would read to me at night after my bath a picture-book story and when he was home, sometimes Daddy would read to me too, his weight heavy on the edge of the bed (but Daddy had to be *in the mood* Mommy warned, which was not always so) and I would see lights skimming at me like butterflies which meant I was drifting into sleep, so happy.

There was nothing that Jenna did then that was wrong or bad.

There was nothing that Jenna did that was evil.

There was nothing that Jenna did that could hurt another person.

4

. . . what you remember, Jenna? Can you tell us what hap-pened?

On the bridge, Jenna. Before the . . .

. . . before it happened, Jenna? The accident.

Behind my shut eyes there was that other place. The rush-ing girders of the bridge overhead. Something like fire glaring in the sky. I saw my finger punch "CD" and waited for the disc to be rejected another time, which would've provoked me to murmur *Shit!* just soft enough so that Mom wouldn't feel obliged to murmur *Now, Jenna,* in mild rebuke.

I heard the sudden sharp cries of the snow geese. Where were they going? It was almost dark now, the glaring-red eye was shutting. A wet, cold wind made the bridge shudder. You understood that the wind could break any bridge, smash any structure and cause it to shatter to pieces, fall into the river and sink without a trace.

Oh I wanted to fly with them! So bad I wanted to fly with the snow geese but could not get my arms free, my head was tight-bandaged like a mummy's head.

Jenna, try not to fall asleep just yet. Try to keep your eyes open and in focus. Jenna, it's crucial for you to stay awake. . . .

Can you see us, Jenna? Can you see me, Jenna?

Blink your eyes, Jenna. If you can hear us . . .

One of these was a woman's voice. A stranger's voice. I hated it! Wanting to scream, to cry. It was not the voice I wanted.

The wind was so strong rushing at me! I could not catch my breath. I was struggling, kicking. The other geese were flying away from me, no matter how hard I tried I could not keep up with them. Already they were far away on the other side of the river. With every beat of their wings they were becoming smaller.

They were leaving me behind. They had forgotten me.

Wait for me! Wait I cried but they did not hear.

I began to know then that I'd been wrong, I had not been loved. Even *in the blue* I had not been loved. My mother was leaving me with the others, I would never catch up with them now.

I had forgotten the name of the bridge. I had forgotten the name of the river. I knew that these were names familiar to me but I had forgotten them and *her name* I had forgotten and the name of *who I am meant to be* I had forgotten and when I heard the cautious voices, *Jenna? Jenna?* I wanted to kick, to scream, to laugh at such a ridiculous name.

Hands were touching me. Far away, at the edge of my skin.

Hands were gripping me, I hated it. I went very still so they would think there was no one here. I laughed inside the bandages where I was a wizened white mummy thing.

Don't remember. Don't need to remember. Laughing inside the bandages *nobody can make me can't make me!*

There was no Jenna, only just this kicking, laughing thing. Foam rubber hands jabbed a needle into my arm. The soft flesh at the crook of the arm. There were needles that stung because liquid dripped through them into my veins and there were needles that stung because they were drawing blood from my veins. Inside the bandages I was laughing, this was so stupid. *Who cares about Jenna? Let Jenna die. Jenna is to blame for the wreck, let Jenna die.* But no one was listening. I could hear them speaking to one another across my pathetic strapped-down body but they did not hear *me*.

One of them was the woman whose voice wasn't the right voice. I would learn that she was Dr. Currin. The neurologist. I would learn that Dr. Currin-the-neurologist made a crucial decision to go into my skull to reduce the swelling in my brain, and in that way my life was saved.

Saved for what, don't ask.

5

Maria was my favorite of the intensive care nurses. Maria liked *me*.

It was a confused time. I was floating *in the blue* and frankly not paying that much attention. Balloon faces hovering over me. I guess I was supposed to know them. *In the blue* it's easier to float happy and serene and smiling at how silly people are, to care about the things they care about, to look worried, to wipe tears from their faces, hey, it's no big deal, you want to tell them.

In the blue that was how I felt. I was never sad.

But when I wakened, the air was so raw. I was a raggedy old cloth doll battered and banged and wrung and tossed down. I was so tired and so old. Wanting only to return *into the blue* forever.

Maria called me *Jenna* but did not know who I was or was supposed to be. I wanted to think that Maria did not know about the Tappan Zee Bridge. Maria did not blame me for the wreck.

Maria, who wore a small gleaming gold cross on a gold chain around her neck. Maria, who smelled like sweet hand lotion. Maria, with the thick beautiful eyebrows. Soft dark down on her upper lip. A way of smiling and calling me *Jenna* that made my heavy eyelids lift.

Jen-na. Time for breakfast.

Oh, I was hungry!

Maria laughed, I was so hungry. You could see that she liked me for being hungry and eating the way I hadn't been able to eat in a while. Maria gave me extra orange juice to suck through a straw. Ohhh, the orange juice was delicious. And lukewarm bouillon, not so great. But the slick quivery strawberry Jell-O *so delicious.*

The kind of food that *before the wreck* would've made me gag.

Before the wreck was my old, lost life. *Before the wreck* was the other side of the bridge.

6

Head trauma. Brain swelling. Amnesia. Facial lacerations, cracked ribs. Visitors came to peer at the weird wizened mummy thing in the dazzling-white bed. *Ohhh, Jenna.*

In the blue I could hear every word. *In the blue* I could hear every thought. *In the blue* I smiled at Mom's sisters looking so shocked and so sad and silly, like any of it had any meaning, but I could not laugh, such an effort would have torn me open.

Jenna! Oh, honey.

A voice I recognized. Not the voice I wanted.

I wasn't going to hate Mom's sisters. It wasn't their fault Mom was missing from them.

She's asleep. Poor child, look at her. . . .

But she can hear us.

. . . should those containers be emptied? The blood is almost to the top, looks so dark . . .

Her face is so swollen. Oh what if she's scarred!

She will not be scarred. Those are just abrasions. It was the top of her head that struck the windshield.

Jenna? Can you hear us?

This is Aunt Caroline, honey. And Aunt Katie. You've been a very brave girl, honey. And now you're mending, and healing, and you will be all right.

I wanted to laugh. Floating *in the blue* it all seemed so silly.

A wizened mummy thing in a white nightie, who cares? There's a flamy red eye, but it's shut. There's an eye swollen and blackened like a rotted plum, but it's shut. There's an IV tube dripping liquid into the crook of the white-skinned arm. You can't see it, but the mummy thing's head has been shaved. All over the scummy-looking scalp are black stitches over which gauze has been mercifully swathed for the sexy mummy look.

What's really weird is: what looks like two insect antennae dangling from the bandaged ears. Two five-ounce plastic containers fixed to the sides of the mummy thing's head so that blood draining from the stitched wounds in the head and face can drip into the containers through plastic tubes.

Gross! Except *in the blue* it's just funny.

The voices went on. Sad voices, cheering-up voices. Foam

rubber hands, face. I loved my aunts, I guess, but maybe I resented them, for who was missing from them.

. . . he's due to arrive, when?

. . . tomorrow, I think. If I see him . . .

. . . no. That can be avoided.

I didn't want to hear this. I shook my head, made the blood containers rattle. I yanked my arm free of the IV tube. I laughed at the looks on my aunts' faces. Suddenly I was flying above them. *In the blue* I'd lost the beautiful snow geese, but I could fly high enough to get away from my aunts and the wizened mummy thing in the bed. *In the blue* I could breathe, almost.

7

From a distance came the voice, a man's voice. I could barely see him across some kind of ravine, and the wind was blowing his words away. *In the blue* something panicked me, my heart kicked in my chest and I tried to fly away but one of my wings was sprained, I lifted into the air but could not fly, I fell to the ground so heavily that for a long time I could not move.

Faint in astonishment and disbelief came the voice suddenly close.

"Jenna! My God . . ."

The swollen eye cranked open. There was Steve Abbott leaning over my bed.

On Dad's smooth tanned face a look like he'd been kicked in the stomach. The way a man would stare at a precious possession of his, a sports car, for instance, that had been vandalized.

"Jenna? You . . . know me, don't you?"

Both my eyes leaked tears. Something was wrong with the tear ducts, my eyes sprang tears for no reason.

"Can you . . . speak? Jenna?"

Just to breathe was such an effort. Just to keep my eyes open was such an effort. To be polite, to be nice. I was so tired. Yet I managed a smile. Some kind of smile. Or maybe not a smile. The look on Dad's face, he wasn't smiling back.

Eleven months since I'd last seen Dad, when he'd been in New York City on business and "extended" his stay for two full days to "visit" with me.

Three years since he'd left us. Actually three years, five months, seventeen days. The shock of coming home from school to see the moving van in the driveway, movers carrying Dad's things out of the house.

Explaining now that he'd have come to see me immediately, within twenty-four hours, except he'd been traveling on business in the East, he'd been in Tokyo and Hong Kong, he was just unpacking his luggage in the Shanghai Omni Hotel when the terrible news came. . . . Such a long distance, the far side of the earth, and complications had arisen so he'd been unavoidably detained, couldn't get a flight immediately, which was why he hadn't been able to get back in time for . . .

My eyelids were too heavy, I could not keep them open. My bloodshot eyes leaked tears.

In time in time. In time for . . .

I wasn't hearing this. Static mostly. Static issuing from Dad's mouth and static inside my head.

In time for your mother's—

I wasn't hearing this! Trying desperately to lift myself, to escape. Except my arm, or my wing, my wing-arm, something was wrong, and it weighed heavy as lead. All that side of my body, numb and dead as lead.

A nursery tune came into my head, to make me smile.

Numb Dead Lead
Say Saying Said

"—and to see you, honey. I've been just devastated to hear of what happened to you but—"

His daughter, this wizened mummy thing?

"—when you are well again. Strong enough to travel. Come live with us, Jenna. There's plenty of room—"

Us. Come live with *us.*

"—would you like that, honey? Poor girl, say yes."

Poor girl! I felt Dad fumble to touch me, not very convincingly.

". . . your room, waiting for you. Our new house is lovely, just a half block from the ocean. Remember, the time you visited you had to concede, La Jolla is 'awesome.'"

Dad was managing to recover from his shock. Or to cover his shock. Dad, who was Steve Abbott, who didn't live with Mom and me any longer for a reason he could not explain except *Things happen in people's lives that can't be helped.* Dad with his tanned smooth melon face and easy smile. Always well dressed, *a man to turn a woman's head* my aunt Katie had said of him, admiring even as she disapproved. Even for this hospital visit, Dad was stylishly dressed. A powder-blue silk Armani tapered shirt tucked into dove-gray trousers, open at the throat. His hair was thicker than I remembered.

Now there was talk of La Jolla, where you never needed to wear a coat. Where the sun shone and shone and shone. Where Dad's "new family" lived. Where my room was "waiting" for me. Where in September I could enroll in the La Jolla Academy, which was a "prestigious" private school. Dad had spoken on the phone with my neurologist, who'd estimated at least four weeks' convalescence, which included physical therapy in a rehabilitation center. Still, that would give me time to transfer. For it seemed that Dad's new wife had connections. There was a close family friend or maybe a friend's close family friend who was a trustee of La Jolla Academy whose "influence" could be very helpful.

Again Dad fumbled to touch me. To take my hand.

It was a raggedy doll hand, limp and chill and unresisting.

It was not a hand that could shut into a fist. It was not a hand poised to hit hit hit.

Saying again how sorry he was oh God! How upset! The shock of such news, unbelievable! His first thought had been of me, of course, his relief that I had not been fatally injured, then the shock sank in, poor Lisbeth. (At last Dad managed to say Mom's name. It came out hurried and hollow, like a word phonetically pronounced.) An inexplicable, tragic accident, a freak accident it seemed, no real witnesses except the other driver, who was in critical condition . . . Dad's words became confused with a ventilator high in the wall above my bed. At all times there was a hum of machines in intensive care. It was a sound of comfort like waves, vibrating air. I was very tired and I wanted to speak to Dad but my throat seemed to have closed up. I was sinking inside the mummy head, where

Dad's words were muffled. *Before the wreck* I had a way of tuning out people but smiling to indicate that I was listening, *after the wreck* it was too much effort to smile.

. . . past two years, or has it been three . . . oh honey, someday you will understand. I was not a perfect father, by your mother's standards certainly. I did not mean to be cruel, it was more that I became confused, thoughtless. . . . When you are older, Jenna, you will understand, though I am not making excuses for myself, one day you will see how you can fall out of love and it isn't your fault or anyone's fault, it is just something that happens when people begin to grow apart in marriage and when they fall in love with someone else, it's like an accident too, no one's fault, and honey, it never had a thing to do with you, in fact it was for your sake I stayed with your mother as long as I did, she told me you blamed yourself, now, honey, you must never think such a thought, *I hope your mother did not encourage you to think such a ridiculous thought, you know your daddy loves you, honey, just get well, honey, please, darling, they tell me you've been such a brave girl, I will make it up to you, I promise.*

I wasn't hearing this. *In the blue* I was spared the words of strangers. The shadow of a giant hawk fell upon me. Wide-winged hawks soaring high above the river, spiraling downward to catch their prey. I shuddered and shrank away. Dad was leaning over my bed to kiss my forehead. Not wanting to peer too closely at the IV drip in my hand, my arm bruised and yellow from needles. Not wanting to peer too closely into the bloodshot eyes.

When he kissed me, I shrank from him.

". . . touch me! No . . ."

My voice was a croak. But it was a voice.

The first time I'd spoken aloud since the wreck.

8

In the blue I flew on outstretched wings. *In the blue* I floated light as a feather. *In the blue* I laughed at the look on Dad's face.

See, Dad, I don't need you now. Mom and I needed you before the wreck but not now.

9

"Jenna, hey. You are one hell of a girl."

I guess. I wanted to think so. Dragging my leg, which felt like lead. But I was on my feet, the nurses were amazed. Now I was out of the intensive care unit and in a regular hospital room, and the promise was I would be discharged from the hospital soon.

I wasn't spending so much time *in the blue* now. Only at night.

Everyone marveled at how I was "improving," "mending." Three times a day "up and about" walking in the corridor outside my room to prevent "muscular atrophy."

Maria's eyes shone. Maria was my big sister.

Lifting me from the wheelchair, getting me on my feet, and helping me walk. The damn IV needle was still stuck in my arm, had to be pulled along on a pole. Talk about *weird*.

In the corridor we passed other patients up and about pulling their IVs with them. Mostly they were older. Some of them had become soft-looking like rag dolls. Even the men moved with such caution, you knew they were waiting for pain to strike them like lightning.

"Jenna, hello."

"Why, Jenna, aren't you looking good?"

I tried to remember their names. Older people, adults, their names just drifted past me unless I kept meeting them or had to know who they were, like teachers.

I was impressed with Maria: She had muscles. Arm and shoulder muscles compact and hard.

My leg muscles were hard from running. *Before the wreck* I'd tried to run every day, but *after the wreck* the thought of running was a joke.

"You go, girl! One hell of a girl."

"Oh, sure. *One hell.*"

It hurt when I laughed, like shattered glass being shaken inside my chest.

Since I'd told my father I didn't know him, didn't want him to kiss me, I'd been feeling stronger. My eyesight was coming back, except when I got tired.

S L O W was how we walked, Maria and me. The hospital floor was like a city block you could walk around, turning each corner until you arrived back where you'd started.

In the blue I'd been spared this. Leaning on Maria like some broke-back old thing, panting through my mouth. Trying not to see how strangers stared at me.

Wanting to say, "Think I look bad now? You should've seen me when they pulled me from the wreck."

In the blue no one ever looked at me with pity.

In the blue the light was always soft. Out here everything was bright-glaring and felt like sandpaper.

"Try not to breathe through your mouth, Jenna. Let's rest for a minute. Deep breaths now. C'mon!"

Mom used to say, "I wish you weren't an only child."

I wanted to tell Maria I loved her. I wanted to ask Maria to be my friend not just for now but always.

Except I remembered: *After the wreck* I wasn't going to like anybody ever again.

Why? Because they fly away and leave you alone.

Too risky.

Such a feeling of sadness came over me. I couldn't love Maria anyway, that was ridiculous. Couldn't return to the track team even as the weakest runner, that was more ridiculous.

I'd almost made it back to my room, but my legs became weak, and I had to sit in the wheelchair. My face was flushed, I could feel blood vessels pounding inside my ugly shaved head. Maria was going on about how well I'd done, how each day I was definitely improving, the gold cross winked just above the V-neck of her white uniform, and I heard myself say, "You don't have to be nice to me, Maria. Unless it's your job."

10

People came to visit. Now that I was out of intensive care.

Now that I wasn't so freaky-awful to look at. So piteous.

Girl friends. A few guys. Some of my teachers. Meghan Ryder, the girls' track team coach.

Bringing me hurt-girl gifts: flowers, candy, stuffed animals, paperback books in balloon colors.

Lots of relatives. (From Mom's side of the family mostly.)

Ms. Ryder gripped my hand in her superstrong hand. She smiled so you could see the strain in her cheeks like rubber being stretched. On the track team we'd speculated on how old Meghan Ryder was, some of us thinking twenty-five? -six?—and some of us thinking older, like thirty?—and seeing Ms. Ryder trying to smile at me now and the puckers at the sides of her eyes, I had to think older. She told me in a bright, forced voice that I'd be walking again, I'd be running again, she was sure.

Physiotherapy, Ms. Ryder said.

Physiotherapy is the secret. Works miracles.

Smile smile! My mouth got tired from the strain. Maybe it wasn't my mouth but my visitors' mouths. Maybe I got tired from watching their mouths. Maybe I got tired from seeing their pitying eyes.

Aunt Caroline saw. Aunt Caroline seemed to be in charge. When she saw that I was becoming tired, she asked my visitors to leave.

Sometimes I just shut my eyes. Tuned them out. A guy from my English class, we were kind of friends, not boyfriend/girlfriend, but I guess I had a crush on him, there he was visiting me in the hospital nervous and not knowing what to say, and I wasn't going to help him, I shut my eyes, suddenly seeing the snow geese high in the sky disappearing *into the blue* and I was desperate to join them.

When I opened my eyes, it was later. A nurse's aide was informing me: time to draw blood.

In the blue was my happiest time. *In the blue* was waiting when I shut my eyes.

". . . try to stay awake, honey? Dr. Currin says . . ."

Aunt Caroline was Mom's good friend. Not just her sister.

30

The two of them laughing together saying how, growing up, they'd had to form an alliance against their oldest sister, Katie: The Bossy One.

I was confused, not remembering clearly where my aunt lived. Mom and I had visited her. . . . In New Hampshire, a hilly drive. Rivers, bridges. Lakes. A long skinny lake that on maps looks vertical. She was staying in our house now, she said. So that she could visit me in the hospital every day. So that she could "oversee" things. Sitting beside my bed, sometimes just holding my hand, and we didn't talk and there was a feeling of Mom coming into the room breathless and surprised-smiling, seeing Aunt Caroline and me together, saying to my aunt, *Oh, Carrie, how'd you get here before me!*

Uncle Dwight came to see me. My little cousins Becky and Mikey.

Aunt Caroline held my hand. Aunt Caroline wiped mucus from my nose.

"We'll take care of you, Jenna. If you really don't want to live with your father."

In the blue there wasn't Dad.

In the blue there wasn't Aunt Caroline either.

11

Tell us what you remember, Jenna.

What happened on the Tappan Zee Bridge, Jenna?

Jenna, try. There are no other witnesses . . .

(No other witnesses! In this way I learned that the driver of the truck had not survived.)

There were skid marks from your mother's car in both lanes. Before the car struck the right-lane railing, then careened over into the left lane and that railing. And . . .

The truck's tires were skidding for at least thirty feet before impact. We estimate that the driver was over the speed limit by approximately fifteen miles an hour when he began to brake. . . .

(What kind of truck was it? I wonder. One of those big ugly rigs or something small like a delivery truck? I hadn't seen the truck coming. I don't think so. Hadn't seen the driver through the windshield. I was not going to ask his name, anything about him.)

. . . any of it? Any information you can provide, Jenna. To aid us in our investigation. The question is why . . .

. . . why the car driven by your mother suddenly swerved into the railing to the right. Why did your mother suddenly lose control of her vehicle at the approximate midpoint of the bridge . . . ?

(Lose control! Mom did not lose control! Fuck you, I hate you both.)

We don't want to upset you further, Jenna. You've been through a terrible ordeal and you've been a very brave girl, but until the investigation is satisfactorily completed the insurance claims can't be processed. The medical examiner has theorized . . .

If you could remember, Jenna! You are the only surviving witness to this terrible accident.

(No. There is no witness. No witness who survived.)

12

But I saw it. It was there. I saw.

I would not ask the investigators. I would not ask the investigators a single question. A pale chill mist like a fog had entered my brain. I was so exhausted, I was a raggedy old thrown-away cloth doll. I was not to blame, I had already forgotten why it might have been that I was to blame. I would not think of it. My head ached too much to think of it. My eyes ached from the blinding sun. My skin ached from the lacerations, the stitches. I had already forgotten the baby deer. Or had it been a dog? I don't remember, maybe it had been a dog. A shadow shape like a deer, or a dog. In the lane ahead. A goose that had suddenly fluttered down out of a V formation of geese flying noisily above . . . I had already forgotten, I wasn't to blame. I would not remember crying, *Mom! Watch out!*

And all that followed then.

I would not! And nobody would know.

I would not ask the investigators if anything had been found in the wreckage because I already knew the answer since they had not said anything about finding the body of any creature in the rubble.

Not a baby deer, not a dog, not a goose. Not a thing.

13

"Jenna, I thought you knew? It's Demerol."

"Demerol—what?"

"To control your pain. It drips into your veins through this tube. It's an analgesic, a painkiller."

I was shocked. I guess I was pretty stupid, to be shocked.

Not to have known what anybody would know: *In the blue* was a damn drug high.

Maria explained that Demerol was one of the "opiate derivatives," and I was being taken off of it, gradually. As my pain and discomfort lessened, Dr. Currin was cutting back on my prescription, which was why I'd been having trouble sleeping lately.

"The prescription has to be cut back gradually so that you don't have a reaction, Jenna. But it can't continue, because you'd become addicted. That's the danger with opiate derivatives and why doctors have to be really careful prescribing them."

I was still trying to comprehend this. *In the blue* had been just some neurochemical in my brain? *In the blue*, where I could fly and float and try to find Mom, where I could explain to Mom that truly I'd seen something on the bridge, truly I'd had a reason to scream and clutch at the steering wheel as (maybe) I had, where Mom and I could be together—*in the blue* didn't exist?

Maria was saying, "It's a drug that can be misused. Like all psychotropic drugs. Like heroin and cocaine. When you're around these drugs you appreciate their power, and if you're smart, you don't want to try them, not ever."

I tried to laugh. I was feeling really sick and scared.

Maria went on sounding like a school nurse, saying how nobody should experiment with these drugs because even if you don't become addicted immediately, you start to compare how you feel with the rest of your life: "And nothing will ever be so good again."

There was something wistful in Maria's voice. I had to wonder how much she knew from personal experience.

Now that I was going off Demerol, I began to feel the difference.

In the raw was how the world felt now. My feelings were raw, my thoughts were raw and hurtful like knife blades.

Everything was becoming sharp edges and loud noises to make me flinch, and lights were so bright, I saw more than I wished to see everywhere I looked. And pain, more pain in my muscles, joints, bones, and brain.

In the blue had been my place to hide, now *in the raw* there was nowhere to hide.

14

Nowhere to hide! Aunt Caroline was surprised, the angry tears leaking from my eyes.

Asked me why, and I said I want to go home.

Want to go home *now*.

". . . my own room! I have my own room in my own house and I hate this room, I hate this bed, I hate this place, Mom and I have our own house *I want to go home*."

Quickly Aunt Caroline took my hand, which was balled into a fist, and pried the fingers open, and slid her fingers through mine, and gripped my hand, tight.

"Oh, Jenna. I know."

15

Good news: In three days I would be discharged from Tarrytown General Hospital.

Not-so-good-news: In three days I would be checked into the Tarrytown Rehabilitation Clinic to continue my physical therapy.

". . . will have to be practical, Jenna. You understand the house will have to be sold."

Aunt Katie, grimly satisfied. I hated it that the corners of Aunt Katie's eyes crinkled the way Mom's had. That her eyes, which were not beautiful eyes, were yet the same pale blue flecked with hazel that Mom's beautiful eyes had been.

And there was Aunt Caroline. Her hair was dark blond, streaked wheat, Mom's color before it had begun to go gray.

The three-bedroom Cape Cod clapboard house on Hillsdale Street, Tarrytown, New York. Two blocks inland from the Hudson River. This property, which constituted most of the estate of Lisbeth Abbott, would have to be sold quickly, I was told.

Aunt Katie's husband explained. I avoided calling him Uncle Daniel whenever I could. The man was a tax lawyer, and his eyes glistened with interest only when talk was of money.

But Mom and I live there. That's where Mom and I live.

I was feeling pretty shitty, not in a cooperative mood. I hadn't been a good sport about having my thigh stuck that morning by a clumsy nurse's aide trying to draw blood for the 5,000th blood test. I was *in the raw* big-time now. My voice sounded like sandpaper rubbed against sandpaper. I said that I intended to return to that house, and both my aunts protested I couldn't be serious, I was only fifteen! A minor, not an adult.

Also, the property was "heavily" mortgaged.

Also, money was "badly needed" for hospital and medical expenses. And more, for the rehabilitation clinic. My mother's medical insurance wouldn't cover everything. And the insurance on her life, naming me the beneficiary, was not a very large sum.

I didn't want to hear this! It was like they were criticizing Mom, when she wasn't here to defend herself.

Patiently it was explained to me: My father was my legal guardian.

It was explained to me: So long as I was a minor, I had to do what my father wished.

"Well, I won't. Nobody can make me."

Aunt Caroline said, pleading, "Jenna, don't be ridiculous. Your father has custody of you, now."

"He does *not*. He doesn't love me."

My voice was hot, sullen, whiny. I sounded about ten years old.

"Of course he loves you, Jenna. You mustn't think—"

"He doesn't even know me. Not *me*."

How could they disagree with this? It was an obvious fact.

The adults exchanged glances with one another. Poor Jenna!

"I can't be forced onto a plane, I bet, shackled and hand-cuffed like a prisoner. I can't be forced to move out there, to live with Dad and his 'new family' in the 'prestigious' gated community, where I will be enrolled in the 'prestigious private school.' Mom wouldn't want me to live with them—it isn't fair. I want to stay with . . ."

My voice trailed off. No one spoke. My eyes leaked tears that stung like acid.

Dad was a double-dad now. The new family consisted of

not just the new young redhead wife but the new son too.

I resented this! It was so ridiculous.

Dad didn't much like children, that was no secret. He'd had about all he could do to like *me*. When I was a little girl, I'd wondered why I didn't have any brothers or sisters, and Daddy told me, *You came first, honey. One of you is enough.*

I hadn't known how to interpret this. For a long time I'd wanted to think it meant I was special.

Before the wreck Dad had sent me a packet of snapshots of his "new" house and his "new" family. The split-level Spanish hacienda-type house in La Jolla Heights, three times the size of Mom's house, with a gleaming orange tile roof, palm trees perfect as papier-mâché trees, an inner courtyard with white stucco walls and gorgeous crimson flowers. The sky was very blue but hard-looking like enamel. Not *in the blue*, where you could float and drift and disappear into your thoughts.

Quickly I'd glanced through the snapshots, setting aside those I did not want to see. These I tore into small pieces.

But there was my "new" brother, Porter.

Porter! A ridiculous name for a seven-year-old with a pinched, squirrely face.

It seemed to be the deal, Porter came with the hot redhead wife, Deirdre. The two were a package.

I was about to rip Porter into tiny pieces when his eyes caught at me. I saw in his face the soft, vague wonderment of loss I felt in myself. It was weird—I found myself thinking of that Steven Spielberg movie *AI*, the moony little robot boy searching for his human mother who doesn't love him. Through the inky-blue depths of the ocean and the vaster depths of the universe and eternity the robot boy searches for his beautiful vain earth mother who doesn't love him. And this mother, you can see, is just an ordinary woman caught up in her own petty life, not meriting the boy's eternal devotion.

Not like my mother. Mom was the real thing.

I was trying to explain this to my aunts and to Uncle Daniel, but they didn't seem to understand. If Mom's house was sold, strangers would live in it, not me. No one in the house would remember Mom, or me. "If Mom knew, what would she think? . . ."

Soon after this, visitors' hours were over for the night.

16

Rehab! It's a word that sounds so good, "positive." But when you're "in rehab" it's hell.

In rehab, sometimes I was a pretty mature fifteen-year-old and sometimes I was a bawling fifteen-month-old who cringed and slapped in terror of being touched.

"Jenna. You will never fully recover if . . ."

I will never fully recover anyway. Who's kidding who!

". . . well, Jenna! *That* was excellent."

It was? Why'm I so wrecked then?

The physical therapist assigned to me was named Devon. A six-foot dusky-skinned girl with bristly cornrow braids whom you'd have to look at twice to realize she wasn't a girl but a woman and knew her business.

Devon had allowed me to know that when she'd been my age, or maybe a little older, she'd been an almost-Olympic-level swimmer.

Devon had allowed me to know that she liked me but just possibly didn't trust me. *After the wreck* I seemed to be having that uneasy effect on lots of people.

Devon was all muscles, sleek and feline. One of those husky sinewy felines like lions, not the skinny type like cheetahs.

Mostly Devon praised me. Spoke of my "courage," "athletic ability," "motor coordination." When I didn't collapse into a heap on the floor mat where Devon was leading me through exercises. When I didn't shriek with pain like a cat being killed. When I didn't shove and kick at her like a crazed toddler. When in the shallow end of the toy-size rehab pool I managed to paddle a few yards without gagging and vomiting.

"See, Jenna? You can do it. Better every day, and I don't BS my patients, see?"

Sure you do. It's your job.

Devon said she'd heard from both my aunts ("Real nice, thoughtful ladies, you are so lucky") that I'd been a runner. She could see, from my leg muscles.

After five minutes in the pool I was panting. Couldn't catch my breath. Every muscle, joint, bone in my body ached. I wanted to scream, *This is* after the wreck, *now everything is changed.*

Suddenly I was asking Devon what she knew about the wreck.

If she'd seen anything on TV? Read anything in the paper?

Aunt Caroline and Aunt Katie hadn't shown me any news clippings if they had them. None of my visitors had said a word except to express sympathy for "what happened," "the accident," "this terrible thing." Because I'd lost consciousness when my head struck the windshield, and I'd wakened in the emergency room, I didn't know what had happened after the car struck the right-lane railing and I hadn't wanted to know, but now suddenly I was asking Devon what she knew, and Devon stared at me for a moment, startled, licking her lips like she was nervous, and told me then in a lowered voice that she hadn't seen much about it in the paper because she didn't read the paper every day, but she'd seen some TV footage. My mother's white Honda had been forced through the bridge railing by the impact of the big truck, and there it was, front wheels dangling over the edge of the bridge above the river, and the back part of the car stuck in the wreckage so it couldn't fall over, and within minutes there were emergency vehicles, flashing lights, the Tappan Zee shut to traffic so cars and trucks were backed up on both sides for maybe eight miles. . . . Seeing the look on my face, Devon paused. She was a husky, sinewy cat-girl but not so sure of herself now.

"I maybe shouldn't be telling you this, Jenna. If, like, nobody else has. Maybe it's better for you not to know."

I laughed. I guess it was a laugh. The croaking breathy noise that would come out of a frog's mouth as a heavy foot stomps down on him.

"How long did the car 'dangle over the river,' Devon? Do you know?"

Devon shuddered. "This guy I live with, he wanted to watch. 'Wow,' he said, 'this is like some nightmare,' 'cause when we were seeing it, the car hadn't been pulled up yet. You and your mom were still inside, I guess. Me, I ran out of the room. I wasn't going to watch. I pressed my hands over my ears, too. Didn't want to hear. If that car fell, and the TV picked it up falling into the Hudson River, I did not want to be a witness, *no thanks.*"

Rehab! Sounds so good, "positive." But when you're "in rehab" it's hell.

17

In August Dad returned to Tarrytown to visit me in the rehab clinic.

Smiling, saying I was looking terrific. I was looking like his daughter again.

Saying he hoped I would let him "make it up" to me—the time he'd been gone from my life.

Saying he hoped I would not "hold it against him."

And that I would love my "new family" in La Jolla.

In his fist of a right hand, a bouquet of a half dozen red roses in crinkly cellophane. Those sleek plastic-looking roses with no scent, the cut ends of the stems in ugly little plastic bootees filled with water.

I took the roses from my father. I sniffed the petals that had no scent. I murmured thanks.

I saw the relief in Dad's eyes that I was able to walk again. I'd gained back some of the weight I'd lost. The color had come back into my face. Maybe there would be a few facial scars after all, but you might not notice if you didn't stand too close.

The new wife, Deirdre, hadn't accompanied Dad. She sent me her love.

I said nothing. I had no love to send back to Deirdre.

Dad apologized that Deirdre hadn't come with him, but she was very busy at this time of year. Still, she was thinking of me. She was wondering why my application to transfer to La Jolla Academy hadn't come in yet.

"If you intend to start in the fall. There is a single position being kept open for you, but . . ."

In the clinic the nursing staff liked Steve Abbott. You could see.

Dad was all smiles and cheerful greetings. Dad was so very grateful: His daughter wasn't an embarrassment to him now.

An attendant came to take the plastic-looking roses from me to put in a vase. An attractive woman with a quick bright smile for Mr. Abbott.

I was feeling tired after my afternoon session with Devon, like a rubber doll that had been banged about and kicked. The application to La Jolla Academy hadn't been received by the dean of admissions because it hadn't been sent. My transcript from Tarrytown High hadn't been received because it hadn't been sent. To explain this to Dad felt like too much trouble.

"You don't seem to be giving the future much thought, Jenna, but I *am*."

I murmured yes, I too thought about the future. But it made me tired sometimes, it was so vast.

"So what, Jenna? What did you say?"

I repeated what I'd said. Dad's mouth twitched in a kind of smile. "'Vast.' I don't see what that's got to do with it. We only need to think about the immediate future, the next step in your life. I'd thought you were in agreement with me, about arranging to transfer to—"

Dad glanced at his watch. This visit had to be a quick one, he'd told me. From New York he wasn't flying back to California but to Sydney, Australia. He would be gone for twelve days, and in the meantime Deirdre would be in contact with me. "I've been talking with your aunts, but I really haven't a clear idea what state your mother's finances were in at the time of the"— Dad paused with a look of discomfort—"accident. I'm hoping they were in some sort of order. I tried to help Lisbeth out as best I could, but with my new family and new responsibilities it wasn't easy. At least there is a life insurance policy naming you as beneficiary. And a fully executed will . . ."

Will! I hated that word.

Mom is not dead but in some other place. Where you can't hurt her anymore.

I smiled thinking of this. Maybe in some way it was true.

In La Jolla, Dad was saying, I would continue with out-patient therapy as well as "the other kind." (Mental?) It wouldn't be cheap, but at least the sale of the Tarrytown house would help pay for my treatment.

It was time to depart for JFK. Dad was a man who enjoyed ending visits. The way he glanced at his watch with a prim little frown as if he feared the time yet with a look of satisfaction that time was passing. A final squeeze of the hand, a final kiss. Promising to call, and I must keep my cell phone on, and get busy with the paperwork to La Jolla Academy.

"Dad, please. I'm not transferring."

"What?"

"I'm not transferring to that school. I'm not moving to La Jolla." I swallowed hard. My voice was surprisingly calm. Dad was staring at me as if I'd spoken a garble of foreign words. ". . . can't forgive you. You were cruel to Mom and hurt her more than you needed to, and you hurt me, too. And now you want to make it up. But you can't. This is after the wreck."

Dad was on his feet, hovering over me. There was a shocked

look in his eyes that shifted to that steely-sharp look I remembered. The look signaling *Don't provoke me! Either of you.*

My voice had started shaking. Dad touched my arm and I felt a sudden rush of emotion, a sinking-down sensation, as if I wanted to be hugged by him. Except Dad was saying bitterly, "Your mother turned you against me—of course. *Cruel* is her word. I was trying to be truthful, not a hypocrite. You blame me, but what about your mother? It was her careless driving that caused the accident, killed her and nearly killed you."

I couldn't believe what my father was saying! Blaming Mom for her own death.

"It wasn't Mom's fault, what happened—it was mine. I was to blame."

"Jenna, what? What are you saying?"

"I—I don't know. I think I was to blame. But it wasn't Mom's fault." My throat began to close. I was trembling. I needed to summon strength from some place deep inside me. *In the blue* was lost to me now but I tried to recall what it had been, the sky opening into emptiness, in the distance white geese pumping their wings, lifting out of sight.

Wait for me, take me with you. . . .

Dad was gripping my shoulders, shaking me. My eyes flew open.

Dad was telling me that I was sick, "mentally unbalanced," "in need of psychotherapy."

Somehow I was able to break free of him, of his angry fingers gripping my shoulders. I shoved a chair between us so he couldn't grab me again and hurt me. It was strange how he'd never touched Mom, only me. Shaking me, scolding me, terrifying me so I was too stunned even to cry, with Mom looking on, begging him to let me go, tears glistening on her face. Only if Mom begged, if Mom said the right, placating words, would Dad relent. And I would be free to run away.

I wasn't afraid now—maybe a little afraid—but it was happening so fast. I wasn't even feeling much pain in my legs, pain that made me cry out like a wounded animal when I was led through my exercises.

In a shaky but loud voice I told my father I didn't want to live with him and his new family.

"If you try to force me, I'll run away. I don't love you! Not after what you did to Mom."

Dad's face was flushed and not so handsome now. I could hear his angry breathing. A strand of damp, metallic-looking hair had fallen across his forehead.

"Jenna, all this is hysteria. You're fifteen, you've had a

terrible, traumatic experience. Your mother nearly killed you, and you can't accept *that*. You—"

"I said I don't love you! I don't want you as a father! It's after the wreck now, Dad. You can't hurt me."

The shocked look in Dad's eyes, for once he got it.

18.

Nobody wanted me to know. But I wanted to know.

Sure I was scared. Maybe it was a mistake. But once Devon had told me, I had to know all I could.

My fingers shook as I typed in crucial code words—LISBETH ABBOTT, TAPPAN ZEE, COLLISION—and on my laptop screen came

HEAD-ON COLLISION ON TAPPAN ZEE
LEAVES ONE DEAD, TWO CRITICALLY INJURED
Traffic Backed Up 8 Miles

TARRYTOWN WOMAN, DAUGHTER RESCUED FROM CAR
DANGLING 50 FEET ABOVE HUDSON RIVER
Car, Truck in Head-On Collision

RESCUE WORKERS PULL ACCIDENT VICTIMS TO SAFETY
MOTHER, DAUGHTER TRAPPED IN CAR 40 MINUTES
No Witnesses to Tappan Zee Collision

I stared at the photographs. My eyes were watering badly. It took a while to make out the car grotesquely jutting through the broken railing, front wheels floating in space. It was a nightmare vision from which you couldn't turn your eyes. TV viewers had stared, fascinated. The car was such a wreck, you could not have identified it as a car, let alone my mother's car. You could not see anything beyond the smashed windows. You could not see human shapes inside. The photos had been taken from a police helicopter hovering only a few yards away from the wreck. There must have been a video camera as well. I wondered who the rescue workers were who'd managed to pull my mother and me out of the car in such circumstances, risking their own lives.

Should have died with Mom in the wreck. You know that.

I was staring at the screen when someone touched my shoulder and I looked up. It was Aunt Caroline.

She'd brought me my laptop from home. It had not occurred to her what use I would make of it.

"Oh, Jenna."

Gently Aunt Caroline shut the laptop. I waited for her to reprimand me, but she said nothing, leaning over me to hug me. I guess she was crying. I don't think that I was crying. From outside in the corridor came the voices of strangers.

It was my last day in rehab. From now on my injuries would be secret.

II

At Yarrow Lake

1

After the wreck my injuries would be secret, I was determined. And I'd never be hurt again. I was determined.

2

September 5, 2004. Yarrow Lake, New Hampshire.

Driving into the town of Yarrow Lake (population 11,300), my aunt Caroline asks suddenly if I would like her to swing past the high school where I'll be starting classes next week. My first panicky thought is *No! Not yet*, but Aunt Caroline doesn't register this, like she hasn't been registering most of what I haven't been saying on the five-hour drive from Tarrytown, so we drive past Yarrow Consolidated High School. It's a two-story dull redbrick building with weatherworn white trim and a bell tower set back from the street, playing fields behind it and tennis courts, a decent-looking dirt track, like small-town New England photographs you see on calendars except the foliage here hasn't begun to change yet, early September is warm as summer. Miles away at the horizon are the White Mountains, which are beautiful to look at but not white, not yet anyway, covered in dense pine forests. Aunt

Caroline is enthusiastic about the high school as she's enthusiastic about most things, *trying to be like Mom, like she remembers Mom,* telling me that her husband, Dwight McCarty, graduated from Yarrow High in 1977, loved the school and was captain of the softball team. Why she's telling me these things of long ago I don't know. Why do adults feel they have to tell you every damn thing that floods into their heads on any damn subject, as if the quieter you are, no expression on your face, the more it means you WANT TO HEAR THIS! when in fact you're NOT LISTENING! Except I guess I am listening because I hear my aunt say that girls' sports at the school are supposed to be good. "But thank God, Yarrow isn't obsessed about sports like some high schools in New Hampshire. Here the focus is . . ." Aunt Caroline turns into the school's crescent driveway and cruises through, smiling like a real estate agent hoping to sell a property to a prospective buyer who's just staring, blank and noncommittal. A bronze-gold banner with black letters is stretched across the portico above the front doors:

WELCOME BACK! CLASSES BEGIN SEPT. 8

My heart has begun to pound with dread and resentment. I am so angry, I can't speak.

I miss Tarrytown, I miss my old school. I miss my friends, and my house, and my room. . . . Can't think how I will miss Mom so my mind shuts off in that direction.

In fact I haven't been returning my friends' e-mails. Haven't been returning their calls. Preparing for the move, finishing up my therapy, it's too much effort. Now I'm staring at the facade of Yarrow High. Where I won't know anyone and won't want to know anyone. And no one will want to know me.

"Aunt Caroline, I can't . . . can't do this."

Maybe my voice is muffled, Aunt Caroline doesn't seem to hear.

Like a willful child I'm gripping the car door handle. Wish I could escape by just opening the door, jumping out, and running away.

Except I can't run just yet. I am "mending."

Five hours in the car with my aunt east from Tarrytown and into Connecticut, north into Massachusetts on Route 7, then north and east into Vermont, then New Hampshire across the Connecticut River (where the bridge at Lebanon just about freaked me, I had to shut my eyes tight and bite my lower lip to keep from whimpering), how many times in secret my fingers groped for the door handle. *I could open this door. Unbuckle my seat belt, open the door, and throw myself out before Aunt*

Caroline had a clue what was happening and could stop me.

Just a fantasy. Silly, stupid. I'd never do it.

Wild ideas that flash in and out of my mind like winking lights.

Like my idea of living alone in our house in Tarrytown. My idea that a fifteen-year-old could live alone. Could attend classes at her old school like normal. Like nothing has changed. (Except Mom has gone. Except Dad lives three thousand miles away.) Stupid Demerol dream.

Aunt Katie had informed me in her sharp surprised voice, *Why, Jenna! The house has been sold. We thought you knew.*

Out of nowhere I hear my angry voice: "Maybe I'll buy it back someday. Nobody can stop me."

This time Aunt Caroline hears me say something. Hasn't a clue what I am talking about, so I have to explain about the house, and that's embarrassing. Like I'm asleep with my eyes open. Under the spell of powerful dreams.

"What a good idea!" Aunt Caroline says carefully. "Yes, someday, maybe . . ."

And I'm thinking it isn't just Mom I miss, it's *in the blue.*

"Well. Here we are."

Pulling into the driveway at 339 Plymouth Street. Where

my aunt has lived for as long as I can remember with my uncle, Dwight McCarty, who Mom used to say was a good, kind, decent man. (Maybe Mom spoke of her sister's husband with a wistful air.) Plymouth Street is one of the better residential streets in small-town Yarrow Lake, but the McCartys' house is an old white colonial with rust-colored shutters and a weatherworn brick chimney, one of the smaller houses on the block. For years, in summer, Mom and I have visited my aunt and her family so I'm familiar with the house inside and out, and yet there is something strange about it now, I can't think what. My young cousins Becky (ten) and Mikey (seven or eight) have come running out to greet us, their smiling nanny behind them. Uncle Dwight is still at work, he's an architect with a local firm. The way the children look at me, the way Becky says, sort of shyly, "Hi, Jenna," and Mikey holds back a little, blinking, looking quizzically toward his mother, tells me that my cousins are registering someone missing.

Aunt Caroline has instructed them not to express surprise when they see me, not to ask where is Aunt Lisbeth, for my little cousins have never seen me step away from any vehicle in their driveway except in the presence of their pretty smiling Aunt Lisbeth.

Quickly I stoop to hug Becky, then Mikey. Shutting my eyes tight to prevent tears from leaking down my face.

Afterward I'll think: It isn't just their aunt's absence the children have registered, but something changed in their cousin Jenna. The way I walk as if I'm trying not to feel pain in my back and legs, and my skin that's still sickish white, and something forced and frozen in my face. On the underside of my jaw are thin scars like commas you can only see close up and maybe there's a smell about me still, that sad chemical hospital smell that makes the nostrils pinch.

And maybe I'm hugging them too hard. My little cousins, I'm hugging them like somebody returned from the dead and naturally this is scary to children so young.

Aunt Caroline says gaily, "Becky, Mikey! Be sweethearts and help us carry some of Jenna's things upstairs. You know which room is hers."

3

Don't speak to me don't touch me!

I'm trying to remember that I love them: my "new" family.

Aunt Caroline, Uncle Dwight McCarty. My little cousins Becky and Mikey.

My "new" room, the second-floor guest room where I've usually stayed when Mom and I came to visit the McCartys in the summer. It hits me when I start to unpack and hang things in the closet, the last time I was in this room, a year ago August, while I was unpacking like this Mom was somewhere close by, maybe unpacking in her room or downstairs with Aunt Caroline. . . . The wish came to me hot and angry: *I want that time back!*

I hate this time now. I'm feeling sick, trembling.

My "new" room. Too girly for me. Aunt Caroline has fussed with curtains, some kind of puckered lavender material.

I hate curtains anyway, I'd like to tear them down. The wallpaper design is some shade of lilac, the ceiling is plain white. The floorboards in this old house (Uncle Dwight is proud of the fact that the house dates back to the eighteenth century and the hardwood floors are "authentic") are uneven and splintery—still, I hate shoes when I'm in my own room. I HATE SHOES! Somehow one of my sneakers goes flying across the room, hits a lamp with a frilly shade, and almost knocks it onto the floor. I'm laughing, breathless. I threw a sneaker like it was my arm that did it, muscles in my arm, not *me*.

Aunt Caroline told me, *Take a nap, sweetie. After our long, exhausting drive.*

Aunt Caroline likes to touch me, stroking my shoulder, my hair.

It's what moms do. Can't help it. They see you're hurting, they need to touch. So I have to check the impulse to shrink away.

Even when Mom touched me lots of times, once I wasn't a little girl any longer, I'd sort of shrink away from her. The way a cat does when she isn't in the mood to be petted.

I especially don't want my hair touched. I hate my hair. No wonder Dad stared at me, revulsed.

After the wreck my head was shaved for stitches, and what's growing back has a weird baby curl. It used to be streaked dark blond, now it's a weird silvery brown, like something faded in the sun. Hate to look at myself in the mirror so maybe I'll turn the mirrors in this room backward.

My suitcases, which used to be Mom's suitcases, are open on the canopy bed. Aunt Caroline offered to help me put things away, hang clothes in the closet, no thanks. Out of the big suitcase I've taken framed photos to place around the room: windowsills, bureau top, desktop. Mostly Mom and me, smiling. Mom always looks about the same age but I'm different ages, heights. Weird to see how in the most recent photo Mom and I are about the same height, standing with our arms around each other's waists.

First thing I'll see in the morning. Last thing at night when I switch off the bedside light.

4

"Jenna. How are you, honey . . . ?"

Quickly Uncle Dwight gets to his feet, comes to hug me, kind of awkwardly. I go stiff and still, signaling, *Hey, no need to hug me, I'm a big girl.* Maybe Uncle Dwight is surprised by my frozen-face smile or the smudged white cord cap pulled down tight on my head.

Maybe Uncle Dwight is surprised by the fact that I'm here in his house. That because he's a nice guy, but mostly because he's the husband of my aunt Caroline, he's taken on the role of stepdaddy.

". . . looking good! So happy to see you. . . ."

Must be weird to be somebody's uncle. Just the word *uncle.*

Dwight McCarty, one of those older men with glittery glasses, soft-spoken, "nice." Half the girls I knew at Tarrytown Day, their fathers were like my uncle Dwight, meaning you never gave them more than a glance, you smiled and answered their kind of awkward questions, backed away and escaped and a minute later, if anybody asked, you couldn't remember what they looked like, even whether they were bald or had some hair. My own dad wasn't one of these, which is why Mom and I lost him.

". . . registration is tomorrow—Caroline says she'll be taking you. I guess you know I went to Yarrow High, class of . . ."

Behind my uncle the TV he's been watching is all noise and rushing shapes. It's CNN news, broadcast live from hell. I guess it's the Mideast. Maybe Iraq. Maybe Israel. Another suicide bombing. A truck bombing. Sixteen killed, thirty-two injured. A woman clutching a (wounded? killed?) child against her, screaming except there's no sound, only just the announcer's American voice so excited and earnest: *Insurgent attacks in Baghdad.* Cut to another scene of sirens, leaping flames, capsized trucks, terrified people running in a street, trampling one another in their panic to escape—what? I must be staring at the TV, not hearing a word my uncle is saying, my jaws have begun to tremble in that weird way, my eyes are filled with tears because the sirens are so loud, the sirens hurt, now my aunt Caroline is clutching at my arm, my hand, calling me Jenna, Jenna-honey, but I'm not listening to her either, staring at the blank TV screen now that my uncle has quickly switched it off.

Later I help Aunt Caroline put Mikey to bed. Next is Becky, who wants to stay up later though she's tired and fretful. Next is Jenna, who doesn't actually go to bed, only just quietly shuts the door to her room at ten P.M., insisting to her aunt she's fine.

Except she's imagining she can hear through several walls her uncle whispering of her *The look on her face, hearing those sirens! For a terrible moment I thought she was going to faint or have convulsions.* And Aunt Caroline *We'll have to be careful, Dwight. Try to avoid news like that on TV if you think Jenna is close by. It will take adjustment living with my niece. I told you it wouldn't be easy.*

In the middle of the night I'm awake sweating through my cotton nightgown. Must be the codeine painkiller I'm prescribed to take each night before bed has worn off.

For pain, the label says.

In the middle of the night I'm crouched in the bathroom that opens off my room, anxiously counting how many of the chunky white tablets I have left: only three.

How many refills: zero.

5

. . . in the dream I'm running. Mom is watching me (I seem to know though I can't actually see her) and at first it's the park near our house in Tarrytown, then it's a track, I am running on a dirt track, it's a race I am running in, our track team competing with girls from another Westchester school and Mom is watching somewhere from the sidelines, and I'm so happy I'm able to run fast again without wincing at pain in my knees, or in the small of my back, my feet are flying and my strides are long and assured and I can't see the faces of the other girls running around the track, I'm breathless pushing ahead—ahead!—I'm the front runner!—and in the last stretch my heart is beating hard hard hard and then I'm over the finish line—I am the winner of the half-mile sprint, people are congratulating me, but I need to find Mom, I need Mom to see that I've won my race, these other people are in my way and confusing me, I don't want to be hugged by strangers, but where is Mom, I'm pleading, "Mom? Mom?" and with a jolt I'm awake, it's a morning of bright acid sun pouring through a window and I'm awake somewhere I don't know, somewhere I don't want to be, awake wishing I could sink back into delicious sleep, safely back *into the blue* where I realize now that Mom is lost, but my eyes are wide open now, the codeine has worn off leaving me awake, sickish, and jittery.

Here is the shameful fact: I've never won any half-mile sprint in a school competition. For sure not at Tarrytown Day, where I was just barely on the track team. Mom saw me run a few times but never anything spectacular like in my dream. Always Mom was proud of me even if I came straggling in second to last, but sometimes I wouldn't tell her there was a race, just after-school practice. I loved being on the Tarrytown track team with my friends, but I never cared enough to work really hard like the two or three fastest runners, these were older girls who were sort of fanatics competing for sports scholarships at Ivy League universities, that sure wasn't going to be Jenna Abbott.

Out of bed, on my feet headed for the bathroom I'm feeling kind of shaky. My right knee hurts, and my head. It's as though in my dream I was actually running. Like in my dream I was exerting myself recklessly and will have to pay for it now I'm awake.

A taste as of something brackish comes into my mouth: Tomorrow is the first day of school at Yarrow High.

This morning Aunt Caroline is taking me to meet with the principal.

When I check, the codeine tablets are down to just two.

For pain. One tablet at bedtime.

When I first checked into the rehab clinic, I was taking four or five tablets a day. Even so I had a lot of pain. Gradually the dosage has been cut back, and this is the last refill and I'm trying not to be scared about it.

The doctor at Tarrytown Rehab said codeine is a powerful drug, and when my prescription runs out, that's it. If I have pain, I can take aspirin. *It will be a little tough at first, Jenna, but you'll get used to it,* she said, smiling at me so I began to tremble, guessing what would be in store.

6

Guessing what will be in store just stepping into the high school building and it isn't the first day of classes, only just my appointment with the principal, and already I'm shaking, the palms of my hands are sweaty. Aunt Caroline has linked her arm through mine as if she senses how I'm wanting to run away. ". . . should have had some breakfast, Jenna. As an athlete you must know . . ."

We're early for our eleven-A.M. appointment with Mr. Goddard. Staring into glass display cases in the lobby. Brass trophies, plaques. Photos of sports teams. It's weird how happy people are in photos, mostly always.

Inside, Yarrow High is just a building. Nothing quaint or New England about it. The floor is worn-looking dark tile, and the walls are pale grimy green. The ceiling is lower than you'd expect. The way rows of lockers stretch almost out of sight makes the corners of my eyes pinch.

In Mr. Goddard's waiting room Aunt Caroline glances at me with an anxious smile. All morning I've been quiet. The night before at dinner I wasn't exactly loquacious. It isn't that I'm not wanting to talk to Aunt Caroline, but I can't think of anything that's worth the effort of saying. I'm wearing clean-laundered chinos and a long-sleeved white cotton shirt and the white sailor cap pulled down on my head, the rim partially hiding my eyes. "Maybe, Jenna, you might remove your hat when . . ."

I don't, though. I'm wearing the hat. Mom had one exactly like it, we bought them at a summer place in the Berkshires.

Mr. Goddard is a fattish middle-aged man with a welcoming TV voice. But his eyes are steely, staring at me like he's been warned *This is the freaky girl who killed her mother.*

"Well, Jennifer Abbott! Welcome to . . ."

My aunt and Mr. Goddard do most of the talking. Yarrow Lake is such a small community, naturally they have friends in common. My aunt seems to like Mr. Goddard, and Mr. Goddard seems to like my aunt: He's registering that Dwight McCarty is an architect, and Plymouth Street is a good address.

". . . transcripts appear to be in order. Tarrytown Day is an excellent school, I've been told. And your record is . . ."

Aunt Caroline asks about advanced placement classes, and Mr. Goddard tells her these have been cut back except for seniors, the Yarrow Lake School District has had to trim its budget. Aunt Caroline seems mildly disappointed yet sympathetic.

". . . not a large school, fewer than three hundred fifty students but plenty of talent, brimming with school spirit. Did you happen to see our production of *Romeo and Juliet* last spring, Mrs. McCarty? A columnist for the *Yarrow Lake Journal* compared it to a 'thoroughly professional production.' . . ."

Aunt Caroline didn't see the production but heard "wonderful things" about it.

The adults are looking at me. I think I must have been asked a question. The palms of my hands are sweaty. For a scary moment I can't think where I am or why. Why has Aunt Caroline brought me here? *Mom must be outside in the car if Aunt Caroline is here.*

After tonight, if I can hold off until tonight, there will be just one codeine tablet left.

". . . any questions, Jennifer?"

Any questions! My head is buzzing.

When you wear a grimy white sailor hat with the rim pulled low, there's lots you are spared seeing.

"Thank you, Mr. Goddard. I don't think so."

Somehow, I manage to get the words out. My voice sounds gravelly, as if it hasn't been used in a while. Aunt Caroline glances sidelong at me in relief.

Is the visit ending? The adults are shaking hands. Already I'm out of the office. It occurs to me only now that of course my aunt spoke with Mr. Goddard before this meeting, told him about my mother, my "trauma," my "split" family. How I was coming to live in Yarrow Lake because there was nowhere else for me.

Outside, I'm too restless to get into Aunt Caroline's car. Some fragment of my dream of last night returns to me, a memory of running, the way I used to run. A memory of being happy.

I want that time again! I don't want this time.

Aunt Caroline joins me at the car, smiling happily. What a nice man Mr. Goddard is. How lucky we are that the school district is allowing me to transfer at such a late date.

"Why don't we celebrate, Jenna? Day-before-school outing? I have some errands to do in town, then I can pick up Becky and Mikey, and we can all have lunch at the Lakeside Inn." Aunt Caroline's voice falters just a little, the Lakeside Inn was a favorite of Mom's.

Quickly I tell my aunt that I guess I want to walk for a while.

I don't need a ride back to the house, I tell her. I'm feeling that I want to walk.

Need to get away from you. Need to breathe!

Aunt Caroline is trying not to look hurt. Saying maybe she could join me. There's a lovely wood-chip trail that follows the creek, she could show me. "I need exercise too! Last year I was running fairly regularly, but this year . . . Why don't you come back to the house, Jenna, and I'll change my clothes? I've bought new running shoes."

This is so pathetic. Aunt Caroline practically pleading with me. And I know if I say yes, it will turn out that Becky and Mikey come with us, they're not going to stay home with the nanny while Mommy and Jenna go running in the park.

"Aunt Caroline, I'd like to be alone for a while."

I don't say "I'm sorry." I don't say "thanks."

My sailor hat rim is pulled over my eyes, I can't see my aunt's face. Already I'm walking away, trying not to favor my right knee.

I can feel Aunt Caroline looking after me. Hoping she won't call my name, and she doesn't.

7

"Hey."

I look up, and there's this guy.

This guy I've never seen before, in jeans and a black T-shirt, ropy-muscled arms, black stubble on his jaws and throat, staring at me.

"You hurt?"

I'm swiping at my eyes. Afraid to say anything, I might break into tears.

". . . need some help getting up? Or . . ."

No! Don't need help getting up; really I'm okay.

Kind of twisted my ankle when my knee gave out. He must've seen me wobble and fall. Must've seen I'm alone on the wood-chip trail, nobody else running up behind me.

This lonely place! Except there are voices somewhere close by, laughter, boom-box music.

For a while I was running okay, sort of slow running like

you see some women and older men, panting and puffing and swinging their arms bent awkwardly at their elbows, "jogging" at about a half mile per hour. That's how I was "running" on the wood-chip trail beside Sable Creek when suddenly my right knee felt like the bones were splintering, both my knees gave out, and I crashed down like a bag of wet laundry and my right ankle kind of twisted and I fell hard. I'm just kind of lying here now, panting and biting my lip to keep from crying, listening to my heart beating rapid and panicked, and angry, feeling some kind of disgusting trickle out of my nostrils I'm hoping isn't blood.

"Thanks. I'm okay." My voice sounds like a choked little-doll voice when the battery's running down.

"Yeah? You sure?"

Is he laughing at me? This guy from out of nowhere. He seems about eighteen. Standing maybe ten feet away, fingers hooked in his frayed leather belt. Unshaven black stubble like quills covering his jaws, he looks kind of scary. A few minutes ago I passed some young guys in the park, some girls with them, loud voices, laughter, like they were drinking beer at midday. Heavy metal rock out of a boom box. Motorcycles parked nearby. This guy is with them? A biker? His black T-shirt is too faded to make out the name of the band (I guess it's a band) on the front, but I see what looks like a tattoo on one of his forearms. I'm scared of a guy appearing out of nowhere.

I've pushed myself up partway, on my knees now. Moving with caution so I don't wince visibly with pain. I tell myself this is *after the wreck*, what's a sprained ankle? A throbbing knee? I survived broken bones, a brain concussion, I should be used to pain.

"Now what?"

The unshaven guy is watching me with a skeptical look. Like he doesn't know whether to be sorry for me or laugh at me.

"What do you mean—'now what'?"

"Like, what're you going to do now? You think you can walk?"

"Walk," he says, like it's the punch line of a joke. When it looks like I have all I can do to stand up, cautiously.

I don't have to answer this smart-ass remark. I'm managing to walk, slowly. Trying not to limp or whimper in pain.

"Looks like you sprained that ankle. Maybe you need a ride home."

No! I don't need a ride home.

Limping along, away from this guy who's scrutinizing me too closely. My heart is beating against my ribs. I don't know if

I'm embarrassed, or excited, or angry, or scared. In Tarrytown, which is in close proximity to New York City, if a guy appeared out of nowhere on a trail like this, and a girl was alone, she'd have reason to be scared. Only last year an eighteen-year-old girl jogger was dragged into a wooded area, raped and strangled and left to die in Morningside Heights, near the Hudson River, and whoever did it hasn't been found.

About twenty feet behind me the unshaven guy is trailing after me, whistling through his teeth. I'm supposed to think he was headed in this direction anyway? Or he's following me out of kindness, to see that I really am okay? By this time my face is pounding with heat as in the worst, the very worst and most mortifying half-mile race I ever ran, in ninth grade in my first semester at Tarrytown Day, coming in sixth, which was last, before a crowd of hyperventilating parents, one of whom was my mother. Worse yet, there's a trickle out of my nose (damn, it *is* blood), I'm fumbling for a tissue out of a pocket in my chinos. Can't let this guy see my nose bleeding! Can't let him see how ugly I am, how ridiculous. I can feel how I've sweated through the back of my long-sleeved white cotton shirt and beneath the arms. Hoping I don't smell of my body.

It's almost one thirty P.M. I left Aunt Caroline in the high school parking lot at about eleven thirty A.M. I'm worn out and hungry. Whatever gesture I wanted to make, of independence, self-sufficiency, it's past making now, I just want to go home and soak in a hot bath.

I didn't need my aunt to point out the wood-chip trail beside Sable Creek, a deep, brackish stream that cuts through the town of Yarrow Lake, runs into a state park, and empties into Yarrow Lake about three miles from town. If you're in reasonably good condition, running four miles to the lake and four miles back to my aunt's house wouldn't be much of a big deal, but I guess I'm not in the condition I should be. It's typical of a runner to be in denial that she's been incapacitated, willing herself to believe that in another few minutes, if she keeps trying, the hurt will go away.

Jenna, don't overexert! Take it slow, one day at a time.

This is Devon's warning voice. At the time I rolled my eyes.

"Oh."

A hurt-little-mouse cry comes out of me. Sharp pains in both my ankle and my knee. I have to stop still, really sweating now.

Of course the guy on my trail hears this. He's like a hunter with sharp eyes, ears. He trots past me, giving me a wide-enough berth so I won't be skittish, the way you'd behave with a nervous cat. Then he stops, regarding me with bemused eyes.

Sloe-eyed. Beautiful dark, lustrous eyes on a guy, with dark lashes as thick as a girl's.

He has a kind of hawk face, long and bony cheeked. His eyebrows are so thick, they nearly meet over the bridge of his nose. And his nose is long and narrow, with deep nostrils. Something glitters around his neck: a gold chain. His hair is jet black, and coarse, shaved at the sides and back of his head but longer and sticking up in tufts at the crown. I'm feeling kind of faint, how he's watching me. How alone I am, in my life.

Like he can read my thoughts, he says, "Trying to run on a hurt ankle—that's kind of hopeless, eh?"

I'm gritting my teeth. Is he laughing at me? I pull the rim of my cap down so I don't have to see this stranger's face.

"Don't want a ride anywhere? You're sure?"

No! I mean yes, I'm sure.

"Is there somebody with you in the park? Want me to look for them, so they can come help you?"

Why doesn't he go away and leave me alone? I am so totally embarrassed.

I'm resting most of my weight on my left leg. I feel like a flamingo! My right ankle and knee are pounding with pain. The headache I used to get deep inside my head at the hospital is starting, like a flickering light.

Wish I'd never come out here. Wish I'd gone with my aunt, as she wanted me to. Why can't I be nice to her, and to my uncle? This is my punishment now, what I deserve.

If this stranger has a cell phone, I could ask to use it; I could call my aunt and tell her what has happened—she'd drive out to get me. At the same time I'm thinking, *No! I can't trust him.* He would know that I was alone in this deserted place.

The next thing he says makes me shiver: "I got a cell phone back with my gear. Want to use it?"

Suddenly I'm cold, in spite of being sweaty. My face must be smudged with blood and dirt. I'm still breathing hard, trying not to cry.

He repeats what he said about the cell phone. I'm so confused I can't think how to reply. There's a faint roaring in my ears like a waterfall. I'm thinking how the night before, climbing into the prissy canopy bed, in that room decorated like Martha Stewart where I'll never feel comfortable, I was feeling sorry for myself, hating where I was, and now, in this forlorn place, exhausted, hurting, sick with dread, if I could return safely to that room, *I would be so grateful.*

"You know what you look like? Like somebody who's been in a car crash."

My eyes widen at this, I'm so shocked.

He's laughing, running a hand through his spiky hair. "How'd I know? 'Cause I been in crashes myself. You could say I'm accident-prone. Except the worst one was just last year, on my damn motorcycle, not even speeding, but the front wheel hit gravel and skidded, next thing I knew I was on the ground. Lucky I was wearing my helmet, which I didn't always do. My brains would've been spewed out on the highway."

The way he's talking to me, like he's confiding in me, inviting me to laugh at him, makes me want to trust him. But maybe it's a trick. I smile, just a little. A scared-girl smile meant to evoke sympathy.

"It's the way you move, see. I was watching you. I mean, I wasn't actually watching you, you caught my attention when you fell down. See, you walk like me, like walking on thin ice. After a bad crash you hold yourself tight and stiff like some-body scared as hell of falling through the ice, scared of feeling pain." He demonstrates, hunching his shoulders like an elderly man and walking with an exaggerated stiff gait. This makes me laugh, though I guess it isn't funny.

"Okay. I got the solution."

It's like in an instant the guy has lost interest in me. He's watching a vehicle driving a short distance away where there must be a park road, except it isn't visible from where we're standing. He trots off without a backward glance. I'm left to look after him. Thinking it would serve me right if he abandoned me here.

But what he does is flags the car to a stop, speaks with the driver, explains my situation, asks if she has a cell phone. It turns out that the driver is an athletic-looking woman with two young children, the take-charge type who's happy to hike over to where I'm standing, shivery and forlorn, on the creek embankment, dabbing at my nose with a bloody tissue.

"That boy said you needed to call someone at home? Here's how my cell works."

Lucky I've memorized Aunt Caroline's number. And lucky that Aunt Caroline is back from her errands. Picking up the phone so quickly, her voice so hopeful—"Yes? Hello?"— it's like she has been waiting for this call, and for me.

So grateful I could cry.

8

See, you walk like me. Like walking on thin ice.

Wish I'd been nicer to him. Wish I'd asked his name. Wish I'd thanked him for his kindness. Wish . . .

9

"Jennifer—that's a pretty name. People call you—Jen? Jenny?"

". . . my mom is a good friend of Mrs. McCarty—I guess she's your aunt? Mom was saying . . ."

". . . Tarrytown, you said? What's it, like, a suburb of . . ."

". . . get into Manhattan a lot? Is that what people do, like, can you take a bus, or . . ."

". . . living here all the time now? Or . . ."

". . . friendly here. Really nice kids, mostly. Our teachers are great, too."

"Except . . ."

". . . there's some people . . ."

". . . bikers, druggies. But . . ."

". . . my dad knows Mr. McCarty real well; they were in the same class here . . ."

". . . someone said track? We could use . . ."

". . . girls' sports are cool here. Mostly."

". . . Mr. Farrell, he's weird at first. Don't let him scare you."

". . . Mrs. Terricotte, she's great. But . . ."

". . . so you're living here, like, permanently?"

". . . Ms. Bowen, she's our track coach, she's really cool . . ."

". . . algebra, it can be fun, sort of . . ."

". . . living with your aunt? And Mr. McCarty is, like, your . . ."

Their names are Christa. Melanie. Brooke. Rosalyn. Susan, maybe Suzanne. Their last names flew past me. Why are they being so nice to me, making an effort I can see, like everybody in Yarrow Lake knows about me, an effort like trying to be nice to a crippled kid, somebody with leukemia? My aunt has spoken to her friends (of course—this is what women do) to ask them to ask their daughters to be "nice" to the new girl: *See, she's practically an orphan, her mother was killed in a terrible accident on a bridge it was on TV and in the papers, she was almost killed too.*

"I'm sorry. I don't care to discuss my family. I don't like personal questions. Excuse me."

The looks on their faces, as I shove back my chair, grab my backpack, leave my tray and food, and exit the cafeteria stiff backed and my heart pounding and determined not to limp.

* * *

The codeine has worn off, I'm feeling jittery and shaky.

Hiding in a restroom. Nowhere to go. What's my next class? . . .

Those girls: Christa, Melanie, Brooke . . . The looks on their faces like the cripple-orphan girl suddenly screamed at them.

Why'd Christa jump up to approach me, smiling, inviting me to sit with her and her friends? Christa has the look of a class officer, and her friends are obviously popular girls, A-list girls, their power as popular girls to anoint any girl they wish if they decide she's worthy. *So rude! Like we were prying into her private life when we only meant to be nice.*

I hope my aunt doesn't find out. In a small town like Yarrow Lake, probably she will.

"Ab-bott, Jen-nifer."

Show-offy Mr. Farrell reads my name from the class list in a mock computer voice. He's been reading off names in exaggerated accents like somebody once told him he was funny, which probably he'd believe since everybody in the room is laughing at him, except me. I answer, "Here," I guess so softly Mr. Farrell doesn't hear it, or pretends he doesn't, so he repeats, "Ab-bott, Jen-nifer," in the same flat way but louder now, peering out into the classroom, searching for this Ab-bott person like you'd look for a deaf or retarded person, and naturally this draws laughs. My face is hot with dislike. I want to tell this guy he should try out for Comedy Central. A strange fiery feeling comes over me:

> *don't have to answer to that name*
> *don't have to play this game*

So I don't answer. I don't play the game. Hunched in my desk with the rim of my hat pulled low over my eyes, and all Mr. Farrell can see of my face is it's (maybe) a girl's face shut up tight as a fist.

After a very awkward minute or two, Farrell catches on that this is the "new" girl, this must be "Ab-bott, Jen-nifer." And everybody else in the class catches on too.

Now it's like I *am* retarded. Or "mental." Something special and scary about me. The rest of the period Mr. Farrell avoids looking at me.

I wonder what kind of mark he's made next to my name on the class list.

"Jenna? How was . . ."

Aunt Caroline is eager to be told how my first day was.

Hoping I will confide in her. Expecting to hear how "nice" people were to me. How already I've begun to "make friends." How "terrific" my teachers were. Which activities and clubs and sports I've signed up for. My uncle will want to know too. My little cousins Becky and Mikey are brimming with excitement about their first-day adventures.

Politely I say it was "fine."

My classes were "fine," people were "nice."

". . . guess I don't feel hungry tonight, Aunt Caroline. I have lots of homework. Especially math. I hate math. Maybe I could just have some fruit and yogurt upstairs, okay? Thanks."

Trying not to see my aunt's look of hurt. Upstairs, quietly shutting the door to my room, and when my aunt hesitantly knocks later in the evening, I will pretend I'm asleep.

. . . tight and stiff, like somebody scared of falling through ice, scared of feeling pain. Like me.

10

"Hey."

I look up startled, and it's him.

This time he's smiling like he knows me. Like there's something between us. For a panicky moment I can't catch my breath, my heart is beating so rapidly.

"Guess you got back home safe the other day?"

Yes. I did.

"Ankle's okay?"

I'm blushing, yes. That a stranger should care in the slightest about my ankle is embarrassing.

"You didn't seem like you were from around here the other day. You go to school here?"

I tell him yes, I just started.

"Just moved here?"

"I . . . guess so."

My voice is low and hoarse, and I know this is a weird thing to say. His eyes wander over me. I'm sitting by myself on a crumbling concrete wall at the far end of the parking lot behind Yarrow High. It's the second day of classes, lunch break. I'm avoiding the cafeteria altogether. Going over my math homework is like dragging a comb through snarled hair. Equations dance in my vision like deranged sunbeams. This morning I was aware of people watching me covertly. A few guys stared openly. Out here I'm wearing the grimy white sailor cap pulled low to shield my eyes.

Just when I've stopped expecting to see him, here he is. Maybe in fact I'd forgotten him. For there is nothing at Yarrow Lake Consolidated High School that holds out any promise to me, after the misery of the first day.

Where he's strolled over from, I guess, it's that group of loud-laughing older students hanging out at the other end of the parking lot where somebody's pickup is parked, and some motorcycles. These look to be seniors of a certain type, not exactly what you'd call preppies or jocks—in a city high school they'd be "druggies," but I don't know what they're considered here, at Yarrow Lake—smoking cigarettes and drinking out of cans. (Beer? Would they dare to drink openly behind the high school in broad daylight?) Today in this safer setting, clean-shaven, this guy doesn't seem so menacing, except he scares me anyway, his sharp-boned face, fierce, spiky black hair, the tattoo on his left forearm that looks like a coiled snake (!). There's something gold-glittering in his left earlobe, must be a stud. He's wearing work trousers of some rough fabric like sailcloth, and a long-sleeved black T-shirt with frayed cuffs. I'm having difficulty looking at his face, those long-lashed beautiful eyes.

He's saying, in his sort of teasing way, "Would it be rude to ask your name?" and I say, trying to be relaxed, my voice like sandpaper rubbing sandpaper, "It would not be rude," and he says, "Then I'm asking," and I tell him, swallowing hard, like this is the most crucial utterance I will make since coming to Yarrow Lake, New Hampshire, "Jenna."

"Jen-na." He pronounces the name in two syllables as if it's a foreign sound. "'Jenna No-Last-Name'?"

"You haven't told me your name."

"What I am named, or what I am called?"

Uncertain how to answer this, I tell him whichever.

"Saint-Croix is my name, but *je m'appelle* Crow."

To Saint-Croix he gives a nasal French pronunciation, San-Krwah. I've had enough French to pick up *Je m'appelle* Crow—"I am called Crow."

"'Crow.' That's an ugly, big bird."

"To other crows, a crow is not ugly or especially big."

"A crow is a . . . predator bird?"

"Is it?"

I'm not sure. Really, I don't know anything about crows except they are large, ungainly, raucous, said to be highly intelligent. Possibly crows aren't predators like hawks and eagles. For sure their feathers are pure sleek black, like this guy's spiky hair.

"Crow. People call you that?"

"Some people. Some others, like in my family, call me 'Gabe'—'Gabriel.'" He crinkles his nose as if this is too pretty a name for him. "At school here, even teachers call me Crow because nobody can pronounce Saint-Croix. Nobody in Yarrow Lake mostly."

"Are you French?"

"Me? Hell, no. Do I look French?"

Crow has a way of speaking somewhere between teasing and sincere. His voice is low and gravelly, not like the voice of a typical high school boy. He does look French, sort of. Years ago, before my dad left us, we went to Paris, rented a car, and drove south to Nice. Crow reminds me of people there. He says, "There's relatives of mine in Quebec, but my father crossed the border into Maine, became a U.S. citizen just in time to be drafted to Vietnam. My mother was born here, and so was I."

Crow pronounces "Quebec" with a hard emphasis on the "Q," like "Kay." He's running a big-knuckled hand through his hair, pondering me. His eyes are like warm molasses with a look of bemusement, as if there's something comical about the way I'm sitting here by myself, math text open on my knees, homework papers fluttering in the wind.

The new girl, alone. Hoping to be seen.

"What's that, algebra? Feldman's class?"

"Yes. I hate it."

"You're a sophomore?"

No avoiding it—I tell him yes. I ask if he's a . . .

"Senior. Should've graduated last year, but I lost a year. Like I said, Jenna, I'm accident-prone."

Jenna! The sound of my name in Crow's mouth, the special inflection he gives to the name like it's some kind of music, makes me feel weak.

"So, where'd you say you're from, Jenna?"

"I . . . didn't say."

"So, where?"

"I . . ."

My throat shuts up. I can't speak. I'm feeling panic that in another moment I will blurt out to this guy I don't even know what happened on the bridge. The wreck, and *after the wreck*.

"Go away! Leave me alone."

It's a joke, I realize. Crow's friends are watching. The sexy-cool older guy pretending to be interested in the misfit new girl, hilarious.

I fumble for my backpack, shove my math text inside, and stammer I have to leave. Something flutters from my hand, I don't have time to retrieve it. Crow seems surprised. Maybe he says something, but I don't hear him, blood is pounding in my ears.

"I hate you. Hate you all. Hate this place I'm trapped in."

Stupid buzzer bell ringing for one-o'clock classes. I am so embarrassed and so angry. Thinking that I will walk out of this school and never come back. No one can force me to be a student here where I don't belong just like no one can force me onto an airplane with my father, to go live with him and his "new family" in La Jolla, California.

I can't face my classes. My teachers. Everyone will know. Everyone will be laughing at me.

I'm at my locker, trying to work the lock. So upset I can't remember my combination.

One thing I've learned since the wreck: Nobody can force you to do anything you don't want to do. Even for your own good.

Except: If I walk out of school, my aunt and my uncle will be upset. They won't understand. They will try to reason with me. And Mom, if she knew. I hate this: *I can't let down anyone who loves me.*

So I don't walk out. I don't even hide in one of the girls' restrooms. Instead I trudge upstairs to fifth-period math. Mr. Feldman's class, which I hate. (Are people watching me? Laughing at me? How quickly can word spread through school that Crow made a fool of me out in the parking lot?) I'm just about to step inside Mr. Feldman's classroom when I feel a jab on my shoulder. It's a smirky red-haired guy with a silver wire glittering in his eyebrow. He hands me two crumpled sheets of paper: "Crow says you left this in the parking lot."

My algebra homework.

11

Oh oh oh, help us

No codeine now, but I've been advised to take Tylenol for "pain relief" except I don't dare take as many tablets as my "pain relief" would require, and I've been waking from sweaty dreams at dawn. By the luminous green digital clock at my bedside I see that it is 4:28 A.M. when the dream jolts me awake like a kick in the belly. I'm tangled in bedsheets, my heart is pounding worse than when Crow was laughing at me. It's two nights later, maybe three. This dream is like a hawk's talons sinking into me. My fingers clutching raw at a railing, a bridge railing that has been broken and twisted, I'm desperate to keep from being sucked through the broken place and into empty space. *Oh oh oh, help us,* I'm sobbing, I'm a little girl sobbing, below us the river is rushing black and brackish-smelling, it has sucked away the person I was with, the person behind the wheel of the car, the person I was trying to save

whose face I could not see, my throat is raw with screaming,
Mom! Mom!

Soon afterward, someone knocks on the door of my room.
My aunt asking if I have called her, and I say no.

12

In Yarrow Lake much of my life becomes secret.

Like an iceberg, which they say is nine tenths hidden below the surface of the water. What you see is such a small part of it, you don't have a clue what it actually is.

How was school today, Jenna? is code for *Are you adjusting? Are you going to be "normal"?* and it pisses me off how my aunt and my uncle are always asking. Even my little cousins Becky and Mikey. Their parents have instructed them, *Be nice to Jenna!* so they try, and I love them for trying so transparently only just I'm not in a mood to play big sister to them. Sorry.

A secret life is the sweetest life. Also the safest.

Weekends are family time. (Even if sometimes on a rainy Sunday afternoon Uncle Dwight, the workaholic, slips back to his office at McCarty, Weissman & Associates, Architects, for a few hours before supper.) The McCartys are children-oriented, like almost everyone in Yarrow Lake, as in Tarrytown, so this means the family being together, in good weather on Yarrow Lake, where friends have a sailboat, or bicycling on the Sable Creek trail, or watching Becky play soccer at her school, or going to see *Shrek 2* at the Lakeland Mall and having an early meal afterward at Leaning Tower of Pizza. Family time is a kind of sacred time, so it baffles and hurts the McCartys when Jenna explains politely that she would rather stay home, she has schoolwork, or wants to walk/hike/run by herself, or . . . whatever it is Jenna does in her room with the door shut for hours.

Doesn't Jenna like us, Mommy?

Of course Jenna likes us! What a thing to say!

If she likes us, she'd be happy, wouldn't she? She always seems kind of sad.

But that doesn't mean Jenna doesn't like us, Becky. It just means that Jenna is sad.

Here is a secret.

How when the McCartys leave to go sailing on Yarrow Lake, I immediately go into my aunt and uncle's bathroom to see what drugs they have in their medicine cabinet. So disappointing! Mostly just boring over-the-counter drugs like Bufferin, Advil, Tylenol anybody can buy, plus medication for "hypertension" (Uncle Dwight) and "dyspeptic stomach"

(Aunt Caroline). I was hoping, with my aunt sometimes kind of nervous and edgy, that she was into tranquilizers like Valium (which Mom took for a while after Dad left us), but I guess not.

Except I don't give up the search. Their bathroom is kind of old-fashioned, with a long cabinet counter and drawers filled with stuff, including old prescription drugs, vials with just a few pills remaining, and one of these turns out to be OxyContin, prescribed for Dwight McCarty, *one tablet every three to four hours for pain relief,* and there are four big pills remaining! I'm so excited, I almost drop them.

Figure my uncle will never miss these pills, the prescription was for zero refills in March 1999.

13

"Hey, babe, you bald?"

Trudging upstairs to math class, which is my worst class of the day, I'm jostled by some obnoxious guys grabbing at my grimy sailor cap, yanking it from my head in a burst of hyena laughter and tossing it into the air, and I'm red-faced, furious, and embarrassed, fumbling to retrieve it, except now that it has fallen onto the stairs, people are kicking it and stepping on it, I'm desperate, pleading, "Give it back, give it back, please," and finally the cap is returned to me, a girl has picked it up, slaps dust off it, hands it to me with a pained little smile: "Here, Jennifer."

To my embarrassment, the girl is Christa Shaw. Who seems to feel sorry for me, not hate me.

I can only murmur thanks, pull the hat down on my head, and escape.

*　　*　　*

Wrapped in a wad of aluminum foil, kept in a secret compartment in my backpack, are the last three OxyContin tablets I've been saving for such an emergency. Risking Mr. Feldman's seeing, I take one of the tablets, trying to hide my mouth with my hand, swallowing the big tablet dry, and praying I won't choke or start to cough and be discovered.

14.

Never! Never tell my secrets.

Never tell my aunt how miserable I am at school. How my face shuts up tight as a fist even when a part of me wants to be friendly. How it's so much easier to stare straight ahead than make eye contact in the corridors, at my locker, in classes. How I dread seeing Crow, or his friends who laughed at me. How I dread being called on by Mr. Feldman and Mr. Farrell, who hate me for sitting silent, sullen, down-looking in their classes. How it's getting harder and harder for me to concentrate on schoolwork, even subjects I used to like, history, English, science. How in gym class I can't keep up with the other girls—I'm afraid of feeling pain. And anyway, everything is so trivial. And anyway, I know that I will fail, what's the point of trying? I've gotten dependent upon wearing the grimy sailor cap even indoors, against the "dress code." Anxious that if I don't wear something on my head, people will see the ugly scars in my scalp from the wreck, my hair isn't thick enough to disguise them, this baby-fine hair that I hate, that I'm ashamed anyone might see and think it's mine. And tiny nicks in my skin, in my forehead and on the underside of my jaw that I can't stop running my fingertips over and over. And how hard it is to walk without wincing if my ankle hurts, or my knee. . . . *You know what you look like? Like somebody who's been in a car crash.*

My homeroom teacher, Mrs. Terricotte, takes me out into the hall to ask about my hat. "Jennifer, why? Is there some reason why you are always wearing that hat?" Mrs. Terricotte's pebble-gray eyes are wary. There's something in my face and in the set of my jaw. Maybe she's been warned by Mr. Goddard or by my other teachers. Explaining the reasons for the school dress code. How most of the boys would be wearing baseball caps, reversed on their heads, so there has had to be a regulation against any kind of cap, hat, or scarf, a regulation that was established by the school district years ago . . .

I'm wearing my grimy sailor cap. I will wear my grimy sailor cap. I tell Mrs. Terricotte that I have to wear it, my head was shaved a few months ago, my skull was sawed open to reduce the pressure of cerebral bleeding, my scalp is covered in ugly, ripply scars that my hair isn't thick enough to hide, my voice is low and rapid and almost Mrs. Terricotte can't make out my words, she has to stoop to hear me, it's an awkward moment, she's feeling sorry for me, very likely she has heard about me, why I've come to live with my aunt and uncle, why I have transferred to Yarrow Lake High from a private school in Tarrytown, how lonely I am here, how unhappy, until finally Mrs. Terricotte relents: "Jennifer, I'm so sorry. I didn't realize. Of course wear the hat if you're more comfortable wearing it."

Touching my arm in a gesture of comfort. Warily.

15

Another secret. No one will ever know.

In the local telephone directory I discover two listings:

Saint-Croix, Roland
655 Deer Isle Rd, Yarrow Lake

Saint-Croix, Roland
Carpenter & Cabinetmaker
39 S Main, Yarrow Lake

On a map of Yarrow Lake and vicnity I locate Deer Isle Road north of town. This isn't an area of Yarrow Lake that I know. My aunt and my uncle don't seem to have any friends there. On a Saturday afternoon in early October, kind of windy-blustery and threatening rain, I bicycle approximately a mile and a half to Deer Isle Road and another half mile to locate Crow's house, which surprises me. It's in a mostly rural area of small wood-frame houses and shanties, mobile homes propped up on cement blocks, ramshackle old farmhouses like Crow's, which is set back from the road on a long rutted lane, partly hidden behind a stand of scrubby pines. This time of autumn in New Hampshire, sumac is blazing crimson, goldenrod is blazing in the fields, when the sun is shining it's a kind of dazzling-beautiful setting, but today is sunshine, then clouds, more sunshine and more clouds, windy and unpredictable. At the front of Crow's property is a pasture in which a single swaybacked gray-speckled horse is grazing, her only companion a black goat with a wispy beard. Straddling my bicycle at the end of the rutted driveway, I see the horse and the goat eyeing me with interest. I'm hoping that Crow doesn't suddenly appear in the lane or come up behind me on Deer Isle Road.

"So this is where you live. Crow."

Deer Isle is a romantic name for the potholed blacktop country road leading out of town, away from the upscale neighborhoods near Yarrow Lake. Crow lives in what is called the foothills of the White Mountains. *Poor whites* comes to me, a term I've heard frequently since coming to live in New Hampshire. Worse, *trailer trash.*

At Tarrytown Day almost everyone came from the same sort of background though there were rich girls, even "really rich" girls, among us. At Yarrow High it's surprising how there is such a mixture: jocks, preppies, nerds/dorks, "trailer trash."

Crow's family doesn't live in a trailer, but this Deer Isle Road is trailer territory. I'm thinking, *You're poor! You don't matter.*

I'm ashamed to be thinking this way. I wasn't brought up by my mother to think this way. But Crow hurt me, I need to be avenged. This is a crude kind of revenge, but it's all I have.

By this time the shaggy black goat has trotted to the fence to peer at me closely. His eyes are a luminous gray-glimmering with irises like thin black rods. So strange! Suddenly he opens his jaws and emits a loud bossy *baaa*ing, shoving his snout through the fence in my direction. Like saying, *Hey, I'm hungry. Feed me.* To my alarm, the mare is approaching the fence, too. Back at the farmhouse somebody could be observing.

"Oh, I don't have anything for you. I'm sorry!"

Hurriedly I pedal away. Don't want to be seen. Behind me comes a loud *baa-baa-baa*ing like disappointment.

I'm halfway back home when the sky darkens and rain begins to pelt down. By the time I turn onto Plymouth Street, my flannel shirt and sweater, my jeans, my sailor cap are soaked. But I'm smiling. Don't know why, I'm smiling. When I come dripping into the kitchen, Aunt Caroline scolds: "Jenna, where on earth have you been? Becky said you went out on your bicycle but—why now? When we invite you to come bicycling with us, on beautiful days, you're 'too busy.' When it rains, there you go."

Aunt Caroline isn't scolding exactly. All this while she's dabbing at my wet hair with a towel.

"I was going to visit a friend out in the country," I tell her, breathless. "Except it started raining, so I had to turn back."

16

"Know what they are, those bikers? Trailer-trash meth heads."

These words erupt from Ryan Moeller so vehemently I'm taken by surprise. I know what crystal meth is, but I pretend not to so that Ryan will tell me. She's a big-boned girl with a broad freckled face and a penchant for moral indignation that seems to mark her as older somehow, though she's my age, a sophomore like me, and a loner like me. Ryan first befriended me in Mr. Farrell's class, where, when our vinyl desks are dragged into circle "modules," Ryan and I invariably wind up side by side since no one else is eager to sit with us.

"They snort the stuff or inject it into a vein like heroin. Can you imagine? Ugh."

I tell Ryan no, I can't imagine.

In fact I can. But I don't want to.

Taking pills orally, that seems safe. The way people drink. But any kind of injecting with a needle is scary.

". . . It's supposed to cause brain damage. Every time they use it, brain cells die. The way those bikers behave, Trina Holland especially, you can see it's so." Ryan laughs disdainfully but with an air of excitement, craning her neck to better see into the corner of the parking lot where the bikers are hanging out in their usual territory that's off-limits to anybody else. You can't blame Ryan for being jealous of Trina Holland, who's the most eye-catching of the bikers' girls, ash-blond hair trimmed short as a guy's, a sexy size zero in really tight-fitting jeans, skinny little sweaters, leather boots to the knee, and a heart-shaped face to die for. ". . . her parents have, like, disowned her. First she hooks up with Gil Rathke, practically a known drug dealer, next it's Rust Haber, who follows her around like a lovesick puppy though Rust is vicious as a pit bull with anybody else. Today it looks like T-Man has scored with her—see them fooling around out there? Dis-gusting! How d'you think it starts?"

"What?"

"Being like . . . you know. Trina."

Ryan has folded her arms protectively across her large soft breasts, frowning and shaking her head as if a wrong-size idea has come into it. She wears loose-fitting sweaters over shirts, size-fourteen slacks in careful drab colors like beige and gray.

Her hair is faded brown-red, she has splotches of freckles like rust-colored raindrops on her face and arms.

Ryan means *Like Trina, not-a-virgin.* I think this is what Ryan means, but I don't help her, it isn't a subject I want to discuss.

". . . and Kiki Weaver, she's a sophomore, you see her making out with this senior guy Dubie by her locker? *This morning.*"

I feel my face blush. I'm self-conscious enough eating my lunch in the cafeteria. (It's starting to make me nervous, eating around other people. Why's it so important, such a "custom," to have to eat with other people?)

You'd think that Ryan Moeller and Jennifer Abbott are best friends, sitting together at a table in a far corner of the cafeteria. A table for people like Ryan and me where we can sit with our backs defiantly to the noisy crowd and ignore them. Guys who sit at this table aren't the kind of guys we would wish to speak with, so we ignore them, too.

Why Ryan seems to like me I'm not sure. She is a big, slow, brainy girl with poor motor coordination, which makes gym classes hell for her, rouses her contempt for athletes as well as for sexy girls like Trina Holland. Maybe she places me in a category like her own, whatever that is. Actually half the time I avoid Ryan by avoiding the cafeteria altogether. I avoid Ryan by slipping out of Farrell's class, seeming not to hear her calling, "Jen? Jen—" (I haven't told Ryan that "Jenna" is my true name.) Ryan has invited me to her house after school, but I shrug and tell her thanks, some other time.

Why I'm like this I don't know. Like wearing my grimy sailor cap every day, it just happens. Do I care what people think? These people? At Tarrytown I wasn't like this. I liked my teachers, I had lots of friends. I had close friends even.

Before the wreck. When having friends seemed worth the effort.

Since that day at the start of the school term, Christa Shaw and her friends have kept their distance from me. I guess I'm a little ashamed at how rude I was to them, but lots of times I've had opportunities to apologize and I haven't. Easier to look away, compose my stony face.

Don't feel sorry for me. Don't you dare!

Ryan doesn't have a clue about me. She hadn't better try to pry either.

Watching the bikers outside in the parking lot, I've lost interest in my lunch. When I eat in the cafeteria, it's always the same lunch: fruit–cottage cheese salad. A roll comes with it, plus a pat of butter, which I pass on to Ryan. If the fruit is canned and syrupy, like the repulsive peach slices are today, I scrape it off my plate for Ryan, who seems never to have enough food on her own plate.

I wish I could eat just white food. There's a purity in white.

Plus Diet Coke. I couldn't live without Diet Coke to fill me up, wash down my pills.

If it's one of those depressing days, I will swallow a Tylenol or two, or some Advil, to deaden the ache in my head that seems always to be there, waiting like a dial tone when you lift the receiver. Aspirin washed down with Diet Coke makes my heart kick and jump in a way that's kind of consoling. And there's the one remaining OxyContin tablet, like a gold coin neatly wrapped in aluminum foil, in my backpack.

(Uncle Dwight has never noticed his old painkillers missing. If he does and accuses me, I have rehearsed what I will say to him: If he thinks that I would steal from him, maybe I shouldn't be living in his house.)

Thinking about the painkiller hidden in my backpack.

Wondering how long I can keep from taking it, knowing its effect will last only a few hours, not the rest of my life.

"Ohhh. Look."

Ryan's voice dips with fierce disgust. A biker has just driven into the parking lot, and Trina Holland and the other girls rush to greet him: hugs, kisses. Serious kisses.

Has to be Crow. In his black leather jacket, even wearing gloves.

The way my heart is kicking, it's Crow.

I've told myself how silly I am being. Crow is such a ridiculous name; Gabriel Saint-Croix is even worse. He's what Ryan would call poor white/trailer trash. I know this.

Since the second day of classes—weeks ago now—I haven't seen Crow except at a distance. Seniors' lockers and classes are in another wing of Yarrow High. Though I see Crow's friends frequently, I'm not always sure if Crow is with them because I look quickly away before he can see me. It's the reflex of someone who has recklessly stared into a blinding light and doesn't want to make the same mistake twice.

Sometimes when I think I see Crow, he's alone. Sometimes he's with his friends. It hurts only when I see him with a single girl, leaning close together, laughing and talking like lovers. There is Trina Holland but also Kiki Weaver with her purple-streaked hair. There is a senior named Dolores who's drop-dead gorgeous like Jennifer Lopez. And other girls whose names I don't know, with pierced ears, noses, eyebrows.

I'm remembering the last time I saw Crow, when I knew it had to be Crow, it was a few days ago, my free study period, which I was spending in the library. I happened to be staring out a second-floor window in one of my zombie moods, not knowing or especially caring where I was, since one place is pretty much like another place, one time is pretty much like another time, and suddenly there was Crow leaving school, running across the grass to the parking lot to his stripped-down Harley-Davidson, not taking time to buckle on his crash helmet before he roared away. As if someone were calling him and it was an emergency.

And I thought, *Wait! Your helmet! You almost killed yourself once.*

Ryan, on her feet to see more clearly what's happening outside, is muttering, incensed, "Oh! Will you just look at that!" After a flurry of excitement it's the ash-blond girl, Trina Holland, chosen by Crow to climb onto the back of his motorcycle, slide her arms around his waist, and hang on tight as Crow drives out of the lot and out of sight.

I grab my tray and walk away without a word. Ryan looks after me, surprised and hurt. I'm feeling too emotional, just want to be alone. The buzzer bell is ringing for one-o'clock classes, and in the commotion in the hall I can be alone, huddling into my locker I can be alone, invisible. In the midst of a classroom I can be alone huddling into my desk. As long as

I don't have to see Crow, and think about Crow, and how it would feel sliding my arms around Crow's waist on the back of that motorcycle, I can be alone . . . and safe.

When I set my tray onto the cafeteria counter, I glance back to see Ryan Moeller still staring out the window, greedily lifting leftovers to her mouth from somebody's plate.

17

Here's why it's crucial to stay alone.

Some stranger crowds in, starts to suck away your oxygen.

Like the Yarrow High girls' gym instructor, Dara Bowen. A dark Indian look, loud lilting voice, loud laughter, a way of clapping her hands like a young girl when somebody sinks a basket, skillfully volleys the volleyball, executes a pretty good dive into the swimming pool.

Bowen is a popular teacher. Popular track/field sports coach.

Not with me, though. Immediately I was wary of Bowen.

Half the girls imitate Bowen's infectious laughter. Not me.

It is said of Dara Bowen she came close to qualifying for the U.S. Olympic team when she played field hockey for U-Mass. She runs every year in the Boston Marathon and has placed among the first twenty women runners.

In Yarrow Lake, population 11,300, that is impressive. An aura about Dara Bowen.

"Jen—is that what people call you?"

People? My shoulders lift in a neutral shrug.

Maybe yes. Maybe no. My wan weak smile suggests *Who cares?*

"Jen. Well. I've heard . . . my friend from college Meghan Ryder . . . your track team coach at . . ."

Meghan Ryder. I'm not prepared to hear this name. I feel like I've been tricked, Ms. Bowen is watching my face for a reaction.

Ms. Ryder. Staring at me from beside my hospital bed. Gripping my hand in her strong fingers, urging me to believe I will walk again, I will run again, physiotherapy can work miracles.

Urging me to believe what her damp pitying eyes seemed not to believe.

". . . on the team, Meghan says . . . until you had, until the accident, then of course, then . . . but still . . . if ever you'd like to talk to me about it, Jen, I'd be happy to . . . do what I can. Also, if you'd like to drop by track practice some afternoon. See how you feel. Meghan recently e-mailed me saying what a terrific team player you were at Tarrytown, how reliable—"

Quickly I say, "I was okay, Ms. Bowen. I wasn't the best."

"You don't have to be the best, Jen. Okay is more than enough."

"At meets, in competition, okay isn't enough."

"Don't think about competition, Jen. Just come out with us sometime. We could use another girl on our team, frankly. How about tomorrow afternoon? Of course, no pressure, you could maybe just hang out a little . . ."

I can't believe this exchange. That I've exposed myself so.

Can't believe I would speak so openly to a stranger who has no right to intrude into my life.

I guess I'm rude, turning to walk away from Ms. Bowen. Not a backward glance. Not a word of apology. Just a wave of my hand, signaling maybe yes, maybe no, maybe *Who cares?*

18

Two days later, something happens.

On the Sable Creek trail crusted with snow something happens. Something doesn't happen. Something that should happen, doesn't. The railroad trestle bridge above the creek. My legs give out, I'm panicked. I can't cross it.

An old wooden trestle bridge. A bridge with a narrow walkway for pedestrians. A smell of wet iron, rotted wood. A smell of winter cold. A smell of snow. A smell of dark churning water rushing beneath the bridge. A smell of froth on the water. A smell of ice at the rocky shore. A smell of sick, sweaty panic. A smell of my body in panic inside my clothes.

This is the first time. This is the first time I have tried to cross any bridge on foot. This is the first time I haven't been in a vehicle driven by my aunt or by my uncle. Since the wreck this is the first time I have not been able to shut my eyes. Like a small child shut my eyes. Like a small child hold myself very still. Hold my breath.

And this bridge! This bridge! A fraction of the size of the Tappan Zee!

The Tappan Zee is three miles. High above the Hudson River, a bridge of three miles. *Three miles.*

A lifetime. A deathtime.

Three miles. And this bridge above Sable Creek is maybe one hundred feet. A wood-plank railroad bridge with a narrow walkway for pedestrians. A sign warns NO MOTORCYCLES.

A sign warns BICYCLES MUST BE WALKED.

A sign warns NO HORSES.

A sign warns CAUTION: TRAIN.

It's a Saturday in November. It's a Saturday alone to myself. Not a family weekend. Not for me. For the McCartys, not for me. It is an alone weekend. Mid-Saturday afternoon. Telling Aunt Caroline I'm going "hiking." In my sailor cap, maroon canvas jacket, jeans, running shoes. Telling Aunt Caroline yes, I prefer to be alone. No, I won't hurt myself. No, I won't run in a desolate area. And I won't go far.

Four miles to Yarrow Lake, four miles back. This is the first time I've even attempted the Sable Creek trail since that first time.

Since falling. Since Crow.

But he won't be there today. If you fall.

Ms. Bowen won't be there. Her fault if you fall.

I never dropped by the gym Thursday afternoon. Not so much as glanced at the runners on the school track. It's a joke. Running, the track team. *After the wreck* most things are jokes.

In secret, on the Sable Creek trail. Liking the way at first my breathing feels SO GOOD. My feet in my running shoes on the snowy wood-chip trail feel SO GOOD. My leg muscles pulling with the strain SO GOOD. To be flying along the ground, swinging my arms. Before I begin to get tired, make the mistake of breathing through my mouth.

My breath is steaming. Panting/steaming.

I'm wearing gloves. Still, my fingers are getting cold.

My running shoes are damp. My wool socks are damp. My breath is coming faster. Can't get my stride, my arms feel wrong. The air feels wrong. A gust of wind blows off my hat, I have to stop to retrieve my hat. The inside of my hat is filthy. The band across my forehead, filthy. My hat should be cleaned. My hat should be replaced. I don't know how to replace my hat. Don't know what happened to Mom's identical hat.

Four miles. Three miles.

So much can happen in a single mile.

Suddenly I see the bridge ahead. I'm not expecting to see a bridge. It looks as if the running trail continues across the bridge. The first time I didn't come this far on the trail. I'd fallen, I had given up. I was finished. But this time, though I am not running very well, though I am panting, and my arms feel wrong, and my legs feel wrong, I am not going to give up. I see that Sable Creek is wider here. A smaller stream has emptied into Sable Creek, now it's quite a bit wider. Yarrow Lake must be about a mile and a half ahead. This is a desolate stretch of trail. This is a desolate part of the state park. No one is running on the wood-chip trail this afternoon, it's crusted with snow. The air is damp-cold, seeping into your bones. Dry-cold is good; damp-cold is not good.

My breath is coming quick and ragged. I am going to have to cross that bridge. Unless I turn back, I am going to have to cross that bridge. Already I'm winded, climbing to the bridge. The trail is surprisingly steep. The icy snow is slippery. The soles of my running shoes are slippery. At the top I shield my eyes against the sun. It's a cold November sun already slanting in the sky, emitting a stingy light. I look in both directions, not seeing any train in the distance. Not hearing any train. But it could be a trick. It could be a trick to lure a pedestrian out onto the walkway above the creek. I think: *If a train comes while I'm crossing this bridge, it will be my punishment for Mom.*

I am going to walk, not run, across the bridge. It is an old shaky bridge from a long-ago time. The walkway is raw planks! Between the planks you can see the water rushing below. The water is frothy and dark. It is like a river here, not a creek. There has been rain, now the water level is high. Broken tree limbs, leaves, and debris in strange shapes like small drowned creatures rushing below. Suddenly I feel dizzy. It's terrifying to me. There is only one railing on the outside of the walkway, and this railing comes to about my waist. This is a railing you could fall over. This is a railing coated with rust. There is a strong smell of iron rust. The railroad tracks, the railroad ties, look rusted, too.

The guy named Rust. That is his name. Handing me two sheets of crumpled paper.

Crow says you left this in the parking lot.

He was laughing at me. In the parking lot they were laughing at me. They weren't laughing at me if Crow was my friend. But maybe Crow wasn't my friend. Maybe Crow was pretending. Maybe Crow felt sorry for me. It's like the wreck. Just before the wreck. I try to know what happened, but I can't know. My head hurts when I try to think. My eyes turn watery,

I can't see. I saw it—I think! In our lane of traffic on the Tappan Zee Bridge. Just ahead of Mom's car. It was a living creature. I saw! Through the windshield I saw as I punched "CD." I began to scream, *Mom, watch out!* My left hand leaped to the steering wheel. I think my hand did this. I think that Mom tried to push my hand away. I think that I screamed. I heard a scream. I heard two screams.

Sirens! I heard sirens.

"I can't. Can't do this. . . ."

Panic is coming so strong, in waves up through the loose-fitting planks of the walkway. A panic I can taste like brackish water. A panic that makes my heart pound in my chest like something with a broken wing. I have to turn back. I haven't gone more than a few yards across the walkway. Not a third of the way across. I have to turn back, clutching at the railing to stay on my feet.

See, you walk like me, like walking on thin ice. After a bad crash scared of falling through the ice, scared of feeling . . .

"Jenna!"

An hour later I'm limping along a narrow blacktop road just outside the park. It's begun to snow, light, feathery flurries that melt when they touch my face. Not running now and very tired. Even my panic has faded. I glance up, squinting through the snow flurries, seeing a car's headlights, a car approaching and braking to a stop beside me. Uncle Dwight lowers the window. "Jenna! Thank God! Get in."

It's four thirty, nearing dusk. My uncle and my aunt Caroline have driven out to look for me. They've been driving on Post Road, on Lakeview Road, on Rockhill Road, Ferry Road. They've been driving into the deserted state park. Aunt Caroline climbs out of the car to hug me. I feel her love for me in her trembling arms. "Oh, Jenna. You've been gone for hours, we were so afraid." Still and stiff in my aunt's arms, my teeth chattering with cold, I don't ask, *Afraid of what?*

19

"See, people come into your life for a reason. They might not
know it themselves, why. You might not know it. But there's a
reason. There has to be."

How Trina Holland comes into my life. And almost wrecks
my life.

It happens by such chance. I mean, it feels like chance. A
few days after the railroad trestle bridge. When I'm still feeling shaky. Worse than ever I hate the buzzer bells at school.
(Teachers hate them too. I've seen them in the hall, wincing
and rolling their eyes when the damned buzzers go off.) This
time the bell is ringing for sixth-period classes. My legs feel
like lead on the stairs. Used to be I liked classes: now, never.
Guys jostle me, maybe on purpose. Nobody teases, *Babe, you
bald?* any longer or grabs at my cap like (maybe) they feel
sorry for me. Or (maybe) they're afraid of me like you'd be

afraid of a sulky cat that could lash out at you with her claws. I'm feeling jittery. I'm feeling resentful. There's a wildness in me, I want to RUN RUN RUN. Even if my body isn't ready yet, I want to RUN RUN RUN. But here I am trapped. In Yarrow High I am trapped. There is nowhere in the world I want to be less than I want to be in Smart-Ass Farrell's classroom where he will be handing back our three-page written assignments on *Of Mice and Men* with his usual sardonic/sarcastic comments making the class laugh like stupid hyenas. Last time Farrell handed back papers, he turned to me suddenly, saying, "Jen-nifer Abbott. Would you read your exemplary paper to the class?" sort of smirking down his nose at me, and I hunched over my desk like an animal that's wounded and dangerous, like I could lash out at him or at anyone who laughed at me. And I would not respond. And it was very quiet in the room, until finally Farrell shrugged and winked to rouse laughter from the class and turned to someone else.

Exemplary. My paper was covered with red scrawls like little scratches. And there was no grade, just "???."

Meaning that I should rewrite. But I didn't.

So, somehow, I'm not going to English & Communication Arts. Instead I'm in the girls' restroom on the second floor of the building, which is a restroom in the senior wing. Nowhere near Farrell's classroom. Out of bounds for sophomore girls. The seniors would give you dirty looks if they saw you coming in here, make cutting comments. But it's empty now, I think. I need another Tylenol, to take the edge off my nerves. I've had two or three already today, washed down with Diet Coke, so my stomach feels bloated. I'm fumbling in my backpack for the bottle when I hear a sound of gagging and vomiting, coming from one of the toilet stalls. Such an ugly sound like anguish, like sobbing. My impulse is to walk quickly out, I don't want to be involved, but I hear myself ask, "Excuse me, are you all right? Can I help?" the way Mom would do, or my aunt Caroline. Whoever is inside the stall being sick to her stomach doesn't hear me or ignores me. Then the toilet flushes, and a girl with ash-blond hair dark at the roots staggers out dazed-eyed and wiping her mouth with the back of her hand, muttering to herself: Trina Holland.

Crow's girl. One of Crow's girls.

Trina pushes past me rudely, as if I'm not there. She's shorter than I am even in her knee-high boots with a heel. I'm thin, but she's really skinny, can't weigh more than ninety pounds and is all nerved up, bristling like a cat. Dumps the contents of her shiny zebra-stripe bag onto the counter beside the sink, looking anxiously for something. All kinds of things come tumbling out of Trina's bag: hairbrush, cell phone, a ring of keys; loose cigarettes, loose coins, wadded tissues; a leather wallet, expensive-looking; a broken watch, also expensive-looking; lipstick tubes, liquid makeup, powder compact and mascara, even a tube of toothpaste; emery boards, nail scissors, a paring knife; a part-eaten apple, and a can of diet chocolate. There's a sharp medicinal smell, a bottle of Coricidin cough syrup has leaked out onto Trina's belongings. (This is the cough syrup that's said to produce a "high" if you can swallow enough of it down without gagging.) Trina is furious that the bottle has leaked and throws it dripping in the direction of a trash container except the bottle misses and ricochets against the wall.

"Ohhhhh, man. Ohhhh, help me."

Trina gags again. Trina spits into the sink. Trina is half falling into the sink. She's so hot skinned, I think that my hands might burn touching her. When I catch hold of her arm, help steady her, she shrugs me off, cursing me under her breath: "Damn, who're *you*? Don't know you!" Trina isn't so pretty now. Her skin is sallow and flushed, and a trail of vomit has dribbled down her chin. Her dark-purple lipstick has worn off. Her black mascara has smeared. There's a curved silver pin through her right eyebrow, a tiny silver ring in her nose, another in her lower lip. Her ears are stippled with silver and gold studs. With so much glitter, her small heart-shaped face looks breakable.

She's wearing her usual skintight jeans. A tight black sweater and nothing beneath. I'm shocked to see on her left wrist a tattoo, a coiled green snake with gold glaring little eyes and a tiny red forked tongue.

Crow's tattoo. A smaller version.

Trina is frantically pawing through her things. Whimpering, "Oh man oh man ohhhh man." The cough-syrup high. Maybe this is it. The state she's in, her heart must be racing. Skin hot as fever. She's looking for something to bring her down, I guess. Sees me watching her in the mirror and gives me a pouty little glare though not exactly unfriendly. She locates a toothbrush, tube of toothpaste, turns a faucet on full blast, and begins to brush her teeth. She's frantic doing this too. Like it has to be done, and fast. "See, if you don't clean your mouth after being sick, the puke makes your teeth rot. It's dis-gust-ing." Trina is too nervous, the toothbrush slips from her fingers. She begins to cry, striking her thighs with her little fists. I'm thinking Trina is dangerous in such a state, to others and to herself. But I can't report her. Can't snitch on her. Want to protect her. Instead I say, sort of shyly, "Trina? Maybe I have something to help."

My last OxyContin tablet. Wrapped in aluminum foil, in a secret compartment in my backpack. I've been saving the tablet for an emergency of my own, but Trina Holland is in such need, I offer it to her on the palm of my hand, and her eyes widen at the sight.

"Oh, man. Is that—"

Trina snatches at the OxyContin, pops it into her mouth without a moment's hesitation, and scoops up a handful of water from the faucet to help her swallow it. She's smiling at me like she can't believe her good luck.

"You saved my life, baby. *I love you.*"

As if the OxyContin can have such an immediate effect! Trina throws her arms around my neck, hugs me hard, and kisses me wetly on the side of my mouth. It's a kiss that smells of toothpaste and something sour and sickish beneath, but I don't mind.

In this way Trina Holland and I become friends.

20

Hey, baby, want to hang out? After school meet me back of . . .

For so long there has been nothing. In Yarrow Lake. In New Hampshire. In the house on Plymouth Street. In the girly-decorated room in the brick colonial on Plymouth Street. Nothing happening except in my head somewhere that scares me. Now there is something. There is something-to-happen. It's six months after the wreck. Cell phone rings, and it's Trina.

Cell phone rings, and it's Trina.

Cell phone rings, and (my aunt Caroline is surprised, puzzled, beginning to resent this new friend of mine not known to her, as I edge out of the room speaking excitedly) it's Trina.

Jenna, baby, hey, I am totally sorry, forgot to tell you, oh, hell, if I did, anyway, baby, we're—where are we, Rust?—some-where downtown, it's like five minutes from your house, we can swing around and pick you up just stand out front, baby, there's these guys from Canaan who are just totally cool—

Cell phone rings, it's Trina.

My friend Trina.

Trina Holland, my friend.

I'm like a little kid standing in front of a mirror, trying on some older sister's sexy outfits. Staring, laughing aloud, it's so amazing.

"Trina, hi. This is Jenna. . . ."

Suddenly it happens Trina Holland wants to hang out with *me*.

Introduces me to her friends. (Some of her friends. Not the older guys, who aren't in school. And not Crow, Trina is possessive of him.) If she wants to cut afternoon classes, Trina wants me with her. Hanging out at the mall. Hanging out at Kiki Weaver's house when Kiki's parents are working. Riding in Rust Haber's battered Cherokee, or T-Man's Dodge SUV painted black with red lightning bolts on the sides, listening to heavy metal music turned up so loud your teeth vibrate.

"Jenna baby, c'mon! You are too cool not to, like, try."

Sharing a can of Bud Light with me, foamy beer spilling over her knuckles as she passes it to me in the lurching vehicle. Sharing cigarettes from her mangled pack of

Winstons. Sharing her dope.

I can zone out, I think. Like *in the blue*.

Trina isn't into "hard stuff," she says. Not into "crystal," she says. Mostly she's into smoking dope—weed—and drinking beer with her friends. She's scared of the other, how it makes your heart pound. How it can fry your brain. But dope, weed, pot, the kind T-Man supplies them with, it's really mellow.

Oxys are really, really great but hard to get hold of. So many adults are into Oxys. The only people Trina knows who smoke dope are kids, but adults are seriously into OxyContin, so the price is high.

I tell Trina it's supposed to be really addictive, OxyContin, so maybe that's a good reason too for not taking much of it. Trina looks at me like suddenly she doesn't care for my face, the way my face looks kind of washed out, plain, especially my grimy sailor cap annoys her, so she pulls it off, fluffs up my hair, stares at me critically, drags me to a sink and forces my head under the faucet and wets my hair, brushes my hair with the brush she carries in her zebra-stripe bag, decides it should be bleached ash blond like her own so people looking at us, "See, they'd think we're sisters, like twins except you're taller. You need a makeover, Jenna. Like on TV. I'm in charge."

That's so. Trina is in charge.

*　　*　　*

Trina, who trusts almost no one. Trina trusts me.

That first day, in the girls' restroom. It's "destiny," Trina says. A girl she doesn't know, a girl with no reason to be nice to her, steps forward as her "guardian angel," supplying her with just what's needed to bring her down from a bad high.

"That's the test of a true friend. That's, like, what a saint would do. Jenna baby, I will never forget that."

Jenna is the name I've told Trina. Now to Trina's friends, I am *Jenna*. Nobody else at Yarrow High knows this name.

Ryan Moeller is bug-eyed, seeing us together. Me with Trina Holland. Me!

Trina and her friends don't hang out in the school cafeteria much, but sometimes, if the weather is really bad, they will stay inside at noon and take over a table. The girls drink diet sodas and coffee for a caffeine high. They aren't into eating, since if they eat, they become ravenously hungry and eat too much, have to stick a finger down their throats afterward to bring it back up, and as Trina says, that's disgusting . . . and bad for your teeth. So some days they are there, in the cafeteria, at a crowded noisy table: Trina, Kiki, Dolores, Sandy, other girls I don't know, and big guys like T-Man Dubie, Rust Haber, Roger Nabors. Always I'm hoping to see Crow with them, but it's rare for Crow to eat lunch in the cafeteria. Trina complains that Crow isn't reliable. Crow doesn't show up when you're expecting him. "He's got this family, this cripple dad who was shot up in Vietnam, who's a carpenter or something. You'd think Crow was the only one in that family, how they depend upon him. He's working for his dad half the time. Even his sister, one day she comes home with an actual baby *and leaves it*." Trina is excited and incensed talking about Crow, but if I ask a question, she loses interest and shouts down the table at someone else.

And there's Ryan Moeller in her baggy shirt, sweater, size-fourteen jeans carrying her tray past our table, staring at me like she can't believe her eyes. Quickly I look away. I don't want Trina Holland and her friends to associate me with this sad-fattish sophomore girl drifting by our table alone.

My new life now, with Trina Holland.

Always there's something-to-happen.

21

Cell phone rings, and it's Trina.

Now I'm never lonely. Even alone, I'm not. 'Cause I can call Trina's cell. 'Cause Trina has said for me to call. Anytime. Day or night. Even if Trina doesn't answer, I can leave a message: *Hi, Trina, it's Jenna, just checking in.*

Next time my cell rings, it's Trina.

". . . was saying, you were in some wreck, Jenna? I guess it wasn't the same one Crow was in, though."

Trina is brushing inky black mascara on her eyelashes. She's leaning close to the mirror, almost falling into the mirror. Taking a long drag from her cigarette, she gives it to me to hold. Not a joint but a cigarette. The smoke makes my eyes water, my throat close up.

I'm surprised that Trina would ask this question. As if Trina doesn't know Crow all that well.

I tell her no. The car crash I was in wasn't anywhere around here. It happened last spring.

I'm anxious. I have told Trina too much. But she doesn't ask me about the crash. Like she hasn't been listening. Peering at herself critically in the mirror. Taking another drag on her cigarette, exhaling, and saying, as she's said before, that Crow isn't reliable.

"He's the coolest guy, but. He's been into girls so long you can't, like, make an impression on him, and I hate that. Other guys, you can be special with them. But Crow, he's *sangfroid*, what he calls it—cold-blooded."

I'm not sure what Trina means. If this is French, she's pronouncing it flat, like English: *sangfroyd*.

"Not that he isn't sexy. Oh, man. Crow *is*. But like, afterward. His mind just drifts off. He's got family up in Canada, I guess. He's got some secret kind of life. Like he says he wants to hang out, but he never shows up. Won't give me his cell number either. That's Crow for you. There's older girls after him, in town. Like, in their twenties? Like, married? I swear. Crow smokes weed, but he's off other stuff now, know why? T-Man says Crow almost died, snorting some crystal. Really pure crystal, you know? Maybe you don't, Jenna. Better if you don't. Crow nearly died, and it scared him. He

148

was in with older guys then. They had to take him to the ER, like his heart had stopped? Oh, man. Glad I didn't know Crow then. My friend Gil Rathke—he's really cool, he's older—was saying they were really freaked, Crow wasn't, like, breathing, his buddies kind of panicked and, like, left him off there . . . at the ER . . . sort of, like, on the sidewalk? . . . 'cause, see, they were scared of cops. Crow wasn't pissed at them, I guess—Crow's into, like, forgiving—anyway, they saved his life, Crow says. Weird, I was, like, this little kid then. Sophomore, like you. Seems sooooo long ago." Trina laughs. She has finished with her mascara, and her eyes look really bright, glistening, beautiful. The curved silver pin in her eyebrow is glittering like a fishhook. Her lips are a rich dark plum purple, you can see why a guy would be turned on by them. The little coiled green snake on Trina's wrist looks like its scales are glittering too. Trina sees me admiring the tattoo. "Crow and me, we got our tattoos at the same time. There's a guy out by the lake, a tattoo artist. It's like wearing the same rings, I mean, like wedding bands? 'Cause Crow and Trina, we are close. It only just pisses me off, Crow has such a thing for, like, hurt people. Crippled people and losers." Trina's sharp little chin juts out like she's daring me to disagree.

*   *   *

Hurt. Crippled people and losers. Trina didn't mean this. I
don't think so. Trina Holland is my closest friend, she can't be
wanting to hurt me, can she?

22

Why'd I miss dinner? Why, three times this week?

I'm sullen, sulky. It pisses me off, having to explain like I'm a little kid.

Like adults explain *why*. Like my father ever did.

Oh, man! Like Trina would say, adults fuck you over and never say why.

Why didn't I call home when I knew I was going to be late?

I did. I think I did. My cell wasn't working.

Maybe the battery is low. Whatever.

Why'd somebody call from school? I don't know. I attended all my classes this week. I think I did. Some of my teachers, they are always in my face. It's like they hate me 'cause I'm a transfer.

No, I wasn't drinking beer on school property! I was not.

I was not smoking on school property! If somebody saw me, they are lying.

Aunt Caroline is saying, Jenna, we need to talk. Please.

Aunt Caroline is looking hurt. Aunt Caroline is looking angry.

Uncle Dwight is nervous, asking what's wrong. Jenna, we need to talk.

Damn, I can't make it inside and up the stairs before they hear me. Before they catch me. Smell my breath.

Trina took my sailor cap from me and wouldn't give it back, saying it was ugly. Wish I had it now, to yank down on my head.

Wish Trina were with me now, she'd tell my aunt and my uncle to mind their own business. *F--- off*, Trina would say.

Wild! What Trina would say. I'm trying not to laugh. Buzz at the back of my head. In my mouth beer tastes soooo sour, but once it's swallowed, once that buzz starts . . .

Jenna, please. Look at us, please.

Jenna? What is so funny?

. . . at the mall. With my friends. No, not the guys. Just my girl friends. You don't know them. I said we went to the Cinemax, can't think of the name of the movie. We ate there. At the mall. No, I don't remember. No, I said it was just girls. I said we weren't with guys. Somebody gave us a ride, okay? A ride to the mall. No big deal. How do I know when the mall closes? I'm not checking the time every five minutes. Who's spying on me, whose business is it? I tried to call you, I said. I'm not lying. I worked hard on that paper. It's because I'm a transfer to Yarrow High, which I hate, and they know it. The teachers know it. My English teacher knows it. Any chance he can, he makes fun of me. Stares at me. *Of Mice and Men* by John Steinbeck is a novel that made me anxious, see. I knew how it would end. I knew. I hated it, the feelings that I would have, so I guess I never finished it exactly. I never read the last chapter. Flipping through the novel back to front, I thought: *Anybody's life could be a story you would not know how it ended, except somebody who didn't know you at all might know, flipping through the pages of your life and not even caring.* And that freaked me. So it was hard to write a paper on *Of Mice and Men* like Mr. Smart-Ass Farrell wanted, so I guess I didn't write a paper exactly. Something I printed off the Internet. I don't even remember. Why'd I do it, I told you. I did not cut so many classes. I did not cut gym class. I like gym class. I like my teacher Ms. Bowen. I tried to call you, I said. Not my fault if the cell battery is dead. Not my fault if you don't believe me. If you think I'm lying. If you think I'm lying, maybe I shouldn't be living in this house with you. Maybe I don't deserve to live in this house with you.

If you can't trust me, I mean.

If I can't trust you.

23

"Baby, come *on*."

Trina is laughing at me. The look on my face. The dazed way I'm blinking and staring.

Thinking: *Trina Holland lives here? In this house?*

Trina laughs just a little impatiently. Pinches me like to wake me up. My head's still ringing from high-decibel Metallica pounding inside T-Man's SUV. My eyes are still watery from so much cigarette smoke. And I'm trying not to hiccup from the beer. This house Trina says casually is hers is so surprising to me, so awesome I guess I can't believe it, almost. All this while thinking Trina Holland is what Ryan calls trailer trash, and it turns out that the Hollands' house is twice the size of the McCartys' house—and the Moellers'—and much more expensive.

I guess I'd been picking up that Trina isn't what you'd call poor. From remarks she's made, the kind of spoiled-sounding things a rich girl might say, and the fact that some of Trina's things are expensive, like her boots, which are actual leather, not fake, her wristwatch she keeps losing, her wallet.

We're walking up the driveway to Trina's house. T-Man has let us out on the street. After school we'd been hanging out at the mall with Kiki Weaver, but Kiki's mom came to pick her up, saying we should come with her too, she'd drive us both home, but Trina wasn't in the mood, so luckily we ran into T-Man and his friends. T-Man drives his SUV so fast, laughs, swerving into somebody else's lane and cutting them off, I'm in the backseat, jamming my fists against my mouth, not wanting anybody to know how scared I am, how I'm thinking: *They don't know. They don't know what it is like when the vehicle you are riding in begins to lose control, swerves, and crashes, and when screaming is so raw in your throat, it feels like flame. And that half second when you begin to know you have lost control but can't get it back.* My friends don't know.

It's cold tonight. Our breaths are steaming. There's snow everywhere, but out here by the golf course, on Trina's street with the fancy name, Palmer Woods Pass, there's more snow than in town, now in the dusk it looks sort of bluish, long, graceful hills like dunes, like something sculpted. And Trina's house she doesn't so much as glance at is so beautiful. From the street you can see Christmas lights winking inside: white and blue. A tall Christmas tree in the front window like a display window. Every house I've seen on Palmer Woods Pass is large like the Hollands' house and new-looking, lavishly decorated for Christmas, so it looks like they're floating in an ocean of snow.

I tell Trina her house is beautiful. Trina mumbles what sounds like "Sure." Like she's embarrassed or—who knows why?—pissed at me.

Maybe because it's so obvious? That the house Trina lives in is beautiful? It's like "Well, duh," Trina wants me to know.

Or maybe Trina is embarrassed she's a rich man's daughter. Not like the crowd she hangs with.

Why we're here I'm not sure. Trina's mom kept calling her on her cell, leaving messages more and more frantic: *Trina, where are you? Trina, you know you are grounded until Sunday. Trina, if I don't hear from you, I am going to report you as a runaway to the state police; they will bring you home in a squad car*, which made us all laugh. Trina says her mom is crazy but she'd better check in, calling the cops on her is the kind of crazy thing her mom might do. But when Trina tried to call her mom back, the line was always busy. So T-Man has dropped us off, I'm not sure if he's coming back to pick us up.

If I call Aunt Caroline, she'll be upset, she doesn't like me spending so much time with Trina, not that she knows anything about Trina. When I'm late getting home, Trina advises me how to talk to Aunt Caroline: always calm and polite to get your way, never brattish; adults are waiting for you to be brattish so they can attack. Already I've used the excuse that I'm doing my homework with Trina Holland because her dad has a special computer for research. When I tell Aunt Caroline this, she is always eager to believe.

"Into the belly of the beast, baby. Hold your breath."

Trina keeps nudging me in the back, pushing me forward. We're entering her house by a side door, into a kitchen where lights are dimmed. Just a light above the most beautiful stove I have ever seen, and another light recessed in the ceiling above a breakfast nook. The Hollands' kitchen is twice the size of the McCartys' kitchen, like something you'd see in a showroom. There's a smell here of burn and scorch and a sweetish rancid smell like something has spoiled. The sink is filled with scummy gray water, plates are soaking there, and more plates are stacked on the counter. The door of the dishwasher is down, but the cleaned plates haven't been unloaded.

On a kitchen chair is a messy stack of newspapers, takeout food packages, grocery bags. I step on something that turns out to be a fork. It's weird, in a kitchen so modern and obviously expensive, that trash is accumulating.

Trina kicks the fork across the floor. Pokes me in the back, to keep me moving.

In my ear hissing, "Shhh!" Like we're burglars breaking into Trina's own house.

The house is so large and sprawling, and we hear voices in the distance that might be TV voices or a woman talking on a phone. Trina slips ahead of me now, tugging at my wrist. The air inside the house is hot as a greenhouse. After the freezing air outside, my cheeks burn. The woman's voice is louder, shrill and incredulous as if she's arguing with someone. Trina pulls me to the stairs covered in plush maroon carpeting just as a woman drifts past a doorway into the living room, not noticing us, she's so intent on her cell phone. All I can see of this woman is she's about Aunt Caroline's age, and her hair is a fake-looking jet black fastened around her head in fussy little combs, and she's wearing some kind of silk robe that falls to her ankles and causes her to stumble. Behind her is the living room with a cathedral ceiling, skylights. At the farther end is the twelve-foot Christmas tree decorated in white and blue winking lights.

Trina whispers in my ear, "Come *on*." I'm surprised, she's

pulling me up the stairs with her instead of speaking with her mother. I'd been thinking the purpose of returning to her house was to check in with Mrs. Holland so she wouldn't call the cops on Trina. "I need some things. You stand lookout." Trina is wearing a bulky jacket with a hood, she could be a boy of eleven or twelve. She switches on the light in her room and runs to a closet to rummage through shelves and drawers, tossing things behind her onto the floor. I'm staring at Trina's room. It's large with several windows, but it looks as if a whirlwind has rushed through it. Everywhere underfoot are clothes, underwear, shoes, boots, pillows, schoolbooks, stuffed animals. Trina's pretty white wicker bed hasn't been made, bedclothes and towels are twisted together. There's the sweet smoky smell of pot mixed with a sharper smell like dirty laundry and old sneakers. The walls are almost entirely covered in rock band posters and photos, tacked on top of one another. On the wall above Trina's desk are Polaroid pictures of Crow on his Harley-Davidson, in a black leather jacket, dark glasses. His spiky black hair is longer than I've seen it. He's wearing fingerless black gloves. In one of the pictures, Trina in low-slung jeans and a tiny red halter top is nestled in the crook of Crow's arm, her arm slung around his shoulders.

Trina sees me staring. She says, "Oh, man. That guy is just so totally, totally sexy."

Trina has shoved a few articles of clothing into her jacket pockets—sweater, panties, socks. Plus what looks like a blue plastic Baggie containing something loose.

I don't ask what this is. If Trina wants to tell me, she will.

Coming downstairs, I can see into the living room to the farther end, where the twelve-foot Christmas tree is winking white and blue lights in the window. The Hollands' house is decorated for Christmas like something in a magazine. On the fireplace mantel are sprigs of evergreen. Pots of poinsettias with petals wilting in the heat, more Christmas lights, gilt-framed mirrors. In the midst of this, like somebody drifting in a dream, Trina's mother comes swaying in gripping a cell phone in one hand and a wineglass in the other.

Trina says in a sharp, teasing voice, "Say hi to my mom, Jenna."

Mrs. Holland has stopped dead in her tracks. She's staring and blinking at us as if she's having trouble seeing.

I mumble hello as Trina prods me forward, saying in the same sharp, teasing voice, "Mom, this is my friend Jenna."

"Jenna. Why, hello . . ."

Mrs. Holland squints at me as if my face is supposed to be familiar to her but she can't remember it. The way she's swaying upright reminds me of a cobra I've seen on TV. There is something spade-shaped and flat about her face, like a cobra's. And her eyes are small and close set. Her eyebrows have been plucked thin. Her face is pretty but creased and puffy beneath the eyes, and her hair looks like a glamor wig. What's shocking is the sash of her pink silk kimono is loose, so I can see a ridge of fat at her waist and part of a sagging breast sickly white like a mollusk.

Trina whispers in my ear, reckless now her mother is so close, "'Belly of the beast'—see what I mean?" and slips past me, and past her mother, like a small child daring to run away, leaving her mother and me to stare at each other.

Mrs. Holland is frowning at me, asking what is my name? who are my parents? where do I live? am I in Trina's class at the high school? and I mumble answers, trying to smile politely and not to sound rattled the way I am when Trina plays some trick like this with a guy, practically shoving me into him, dancing away giggling what sounds like *Here's Jenna, she wants to suck your dick,* except you can't be sure what Trina has said, you have to pretend you haven't heard.

(I can't be angry at Trina, she does this with anybody she likes. Even some of the guys. It's how you know Trina Holland likes you, this kind of teasing.)

Mrs. Holland doesn't listen to much of what I say, she's chattering about something in a hurt, girlish voice. I can understand why Trima slipped away. Mrs. Holland's voice would give you a headache in five minutes. She's complaining about Trina, I guess, or about somebody who was supposed to "cater" a party for her but has canceled at the last minute: "She knew this relative was dying, he's been dying for months, it's her professional responsibility to fulfill her obligation to a customer, don't my feelings matter too?"

Mrs. Holland has forgotten she was speaking on the cell phone, she's startled by a shrill little voice squawking out of it, drops the cell phone, grabs at it but misses it, it clatters to the floor and breaks into three pieces, somehow the wineglass slips through her fingers too and shatters on the floor. Mrs. Holland cries, "Oh oh oh! Oh, *no!*" Dark-red wine has splattered up onto the beautiful silk kimono. Nasty-looking pieces of glass are glittering on the marble floor. I don't know where Trina has gone, somewhere in the living room, but for sure, she isn't in a hurry to investigate her mother's cries and what the accident is.

I tell Mrs. Holland it's all right. I'll take care of the broken glass.

Mrs. Holland leans heavily on me as I help her to a chair in a corner of the foyer, sobbing like an infuriated child. The fumes on her breath smell like lighter fluid. I stoop to pick up the pieces of the cell phone, which is now completely silent, and as many pieces of the broken wineglass as I can find, and I mop up the spilled wine with paper napkins. Mrs. Holland doesn't seem to notice; she's peering at me suspiciously, asking suddenly, "Who are *you*? Do I know *you*?"

"I—I'm Jenna. Trina's friend from high school."

"But I don't know you, do I? What are you doing in my house?"

This is scary. I'm wishing that Trina would come back.

I don't even know what to say. *Trina brought me here? Why, I don't know any more than you do, Mrs. Holland.*

Mrs. Holland calls, "Trina? Where are you? Tree-eena!" She's so drunk, it's hard to know if she is furious or sad or her heart is broken or mostly she's just disgusted and wants to blame me.

"Where is my daughter? Why is my daughter always gone? Who are my daughter's friends? All that I've done for that child, why doesn't she love me when I love her so much?" Mrs. Holland is gripping my hand so hard, I have to pry her fingers off, trying not to panic.

"Hey, Mom: chill."

Trina comes sauntering into the foyer, the hood of her jacket pulled up so her face is half covered. She's carrying her backpack, which looks kind of bulky and heavy. "We're leaving now—g'night."

"But—Trina! Don't you have homework? Both of you?"

Trina's walking away, pulling me with her. Like she's talking to some mental defective in a loud flat voice: "Mom, see, I explained. Jenna's dad is this engineering genius, he's got this supernew awesome computer, he lets us use for research? For, like, my earth science class? So—"

We're at the front door. Trina opens it, shoves me out into the cold air, which hits my face like a wall. At first my skin hurts; then I'm grateful for the cold, after the hothouse heat of Mrs. Holland's house. Behind us Trina's mother is calling plaintively for Trina to come back, has Trina forgotten she's grounded all this week—

Trina slams the door shut. Trina's laughing, so I guess things are okay, but halfway up the front walk she turns on me, angry. "Why'd you do that? She's not your mother."

Not my mother. These words hurt. I'm glad Trina takes no notice.

On the snowy street we're waiting for somebody, I guess. Our breaths are steaming. Trina says, relenting, "See, baby, I got the goods." There are several bottles in her backpack, and she pulls one out: Parrot Bay Puerto Rican rum. Trina screws off the top, takes a long swallow, wipes her mouth on her sleeve the way a guy would do, and passes the bottle to me. The liquid is so strong going down, it feels like flame in my mouth, throat, chest. I'm trying not to have a coughing fit when T-Man reappears in his black SUV with the red lightning bolts on the sides, skidding and braking for Trina and me to climb inside.

This is the night Trina says, *Know what, you guys could help me out real well,* and the guys ask how and Trina says, *Kill my mom for me, put the beast out of her misery,* and the guys are like *Whaaaat?* not knowing if they've heard right, and Trina says, laughing, *Just kidding, guys.*

Trina's my friend, I am never lonely now.

24.

Jenna! Come downstairs, honey.

Mom is calling up the stairs. It's Christmas Eve!

Strange that I'm so sleepy. My eyelids feel glued shut. Mom's voice sounds far away. When I try to answer her and run to the stairs, my legs are tangled in something: bedclothes?

Christmas Eve! For days Mom and I have been decorating the tree. So many beautiful ornaments, and some I've made myself in art class. Last week Mom let me pick out the tree at the nursery, a Douglas fir it's called. The needles smell so wonderful, like the fresh air of a forest. Beneath the tree are our presents. I love Christmas presents even more than birthday presents because there are so many of them and because of the way they look in their shining wrapping paper. Like the Christmas tree sparkling and winking with glass ornaments, silver tinsel, red and green colored lights. And the fluffy white angel at the peak.

Each of the presents marked "JENNA" is fascinating to me, like a riddle in one of my picture books when I was a little girl. There are presents from "Mom & Dad," including a big square box that rattles when I shake it—I can't guess what's inside and Mom won't even hint what it is; there are heaps of presents from "Grandma," from "Aunt Caroline & Uncle Dwight," from other relatives. My present for Mom looks kind of small, not much larger than a necktie box. The salesclerk wrapped it in silver paper, but I marked it myself in red ink "TO MOM FROM JENNA." It's a purple velvet shawl sprinkled with gold stars. Daddy took me shopping, but I bought Mom's present with my own money. (Mom helped me buy our present for Daddy, a hand-knit sweater from Scotland. Anything Daddy might really like is so expensive.) So many beautiful shawls the salesclerk showed me, I had a hard time choosing. I asked Daddy to help, but Daddy was talking on his cell phone and didn't want to be interrupted. Like Daddy has other things to think about that mean more to him than buying a Christmas present for Mom.

Jenna? is fading now.

Mom's voice is fading, and I can't open my eyes, can't move my legs. Want to scream, *Mommy, help me! Mommy, don't leave me!* but the words are trapped inside.

25.

"Jenna? We're waiting, honey . . ."

It's Christmas Eve, but another year. Not Mom but Aunt Caroline is calling up the stairs to me. Her voice is eager, hopeful. I am not trapped in a dream, I am awake and hating it.

I can't. I won't. I'm not your daughter.

"BIG Z it's called: 'BZ.' It's really really cool, but don't try to swallow it whole—you will, like, *choke to death*. What I do," Trina says, "is, like, saw it in four chunks with a knife or a scissors or something."

I saw them earlier from the stairway landing. Christmas Eve is Family Time. The house smells of evergreen needles. Becky and Mikey are so excited, they can't sit still. There was Uncle Dwight jabbing burning logs with a poker in the fireplace.

There was Aunt Caroline handing Mikey the first of the heaps of presents to be uwrapped.

It's obvious how happy the McCartys are without me.

I'm a scrawny, sulky girl in patchy jeans, an old Tarrytown T-shirt, and a black pullover. My hair that's so weird and curly, that I hate, is brushed back as flat as I can make it. Last time I looked in a mirror, you could see scars. Like a giant cobweb scar grown over my face.

Jenna? Be nice to them, they love you in my place.

This is what Mom would say. I know.

In my room on my bureau is a picture I love, of Mom smiling and pretty. Other pictures, I'm with Mom at different ages, but I never look at myself, only at Mom. Sometimes I hear Mom's voice as clear as if she's in the room with me. When I run—or try to run—I hear Mom's voice a lot. Other times I'm not sure what I hear.

. . . they love you in my place, Jenna. Please let them.

But I'm not so sure I want to be loved. You just wind up being hurt.

This is my first Christmas without Mom. First Christmas *after the wreck.* I'm lying on my bed feeling like *Whaaat?* like you'd feel in a car smashed through a railing, dangling over a deep rushing river. *Whaaat?* like the stunned goofy looks on the guys' faces when Trina said for them to kill her mom for her, but Trina was only teasing.

You'd have to know Trina to know that she was teasing.

You'd have to be really close to Trina to know that she was teasing. Like I am.

Aunt Caroline is calling my name, wants me to come downstairs for Christmas Eve. If I could reach the door from my bed, I would open it and call down to her, *Be there in a minute, don't wait for me*, but I can't reach the door, it's too much effort.

Whaaat? is kind of a cool sensation like floating/falling. I'm lying on top of my bed arms/legs stretched wide. I sawed the chunky yellow pill Trina's friend Jax gave me, for free, into four crumbling pieces with the edge of my scissors.

I hate being awake. Raw-awake. That hurts. When I tried to tell Trina about Mom and how wonderful it was *in the blue* where I could be with Mom, Trina got excited, asking about Demerol, if I knew anybody on the hospital staff, or the rehab clinic, who could supply me?

Better than Oxys, Trina said. What you hear of Demerol, it's, like, the perfect high.

Now Uncle Dwight is calling up the stairs: "Jenna? We're waiting."

Becky calls: "Jen-na! C'mon!"

I'm supposed to be a big sister to Becky, I guess. Too much effort.

My little cousins Becky and Mikey have been excited about Christmas for what seems like months. I try to think: *They're sweet little kids, I love them.* But the thought just fades. I can't seem to hold on to any thought for very long.

Took all four pieces of the pill before dinner. Earlier today, three or four extra-strength Tylenols with Diet Coke.

What I hate is my stomach bloating, but at least I'm not hungry.

Late afternoon, when I was in the kitchen helping Aunt Caroline prepare Christmas Eve dinner, the phone rang, and it was Dad calling, and I ran away and refused to speak to him, so Aunt Caroline had to, then Uncle Dwight. What Dad wanted to know was did his presents arrive, and why wouldn't Jenna return his calls?

When my cell phone rings, and the ID is just CALIFOR-NIA, I never pick up.

This big Christmas card came from Dad. On the front was a glossy photo of the awesome new Spanish-style house and the new family smiling in the sunshine amid crimson bougainvillea, looking as fake as a movie set. Inside was "*Love from Deirdre, Porter, Dad.*" I don't know if I actually saw this. The card slipped from my fingers onto the floor. Later I overheard my aunt Caroline say to my uncle Dwight, *How could Steve be so insensitive?* and my uncle said, *That's Steve Abbott.*

Like you'd say, well, a scorpion stings.

Family Time. I'm supposed to unwrap my presents. Watch them unwrap theirs. I will say I'm sick to my stomach. (This is true. And I can make myself sicker, I know how.)

Trina hasn't called for six days. Since that night she took me to her house. Said we'd hook up over the break, some guys were having a party out at the lake, but Trina never called, doesn't return my calls to her cell. It's from Kiki Weaver I learned that Trina is in St. Bart's in the Caribbean (!), her family goes every Christmas, and she won't be back until after New Year's.

Sometimes I hate Trina, you can't trust her. What she says is just words.

I miss Trina, though. I bought her a really cool/sexy shimmery-midnight-blue top from Banana Republic and a pair of angora leg warmers, the kind dancers wear.

Suddenly Aunt Caroline's voice sounds closer. Must be on the stairway landing, calling up. "Jenna . . . ?"

I don't want Aunt Caroline coming into my room, so I quickly say, "I'm okay, Aunt Caroline. I'll be down in a . . ." but my voice isn't strong enough, my words fade like air leaking from a balloon.

Why don't they open their presents without me? Nobody really wants *me*.

Actually, I bought Christmas presents. I bought presents for my new family: Aunt Caroline, Uncle Dwight, Becky, and Mikey. (I did not buy a present for my father. I will not open the presents to me from my father.) I watched myself at the mall, saw myself in store windows and mirrors, moving like a ghost. Buying things nobody wants, nobody needs. In my room, wrapping presents so that other people can tear off the wrapping paper.

I still have my present for Trina. Hidden in a drawer in my bureau.

I miss Crow. I have not seen him for a long time except at a distance.

Crow was kind to me. I guess. The way you don't expect a guy to be. Anyway, most guys. Most biker guys for sure. I was the one who was rude, weird-acting. I am so ashamed! I can't seem to control my emotions. *I love Crow* is a stupid shameful fact.

"Why, Jenna. Are you—"

Aunt Caroline has come into my room. If she knocked on my door, I didn't hear.

I'm on the top of my bed where (I guess) I've fallen from some height. Arms/legs spread. Don't know if I am floating or heavy as lead. Trying to say I'm okay, leave me alone, but my voice is slow and hoarse like my tongue is swollen, and my aunt is stooping over me, sitting beside me, touches my forehead with her fingers, so in this instant I think, *This is Mom, I'm a little girl again sick in bed with a fever. Mom is here with me.* For that moment I feel safe, such a warm sensation in my heart.

Stupid Jenna! This isn't Mom, this is my aunt.

Maybe it was a mistake taking all of the Big Z. Maybe should've waited.

Ohhhh, this heavy-sinking feeling inside my head! Not floating like *in the blue*. It's kind of scary, I guess. Seeing my aunt and my uncle staring at me. Wanting to say something, to explain, but I don't know what I am trying to say.

I shut my eyes so that they will go away. It's another time (I think it's a later time), but somebody is still sitting close beside me on the bed, asking in a worried voice, did I take anything? any drug? and I'm trying to explain I just want to sleep, I'm not sick. Someone is saying it's Christmas Eve, it isn't nine o'clock yet, and usually I don't go to bed so early, something must be wrong with me. I'm trying to push the hands away, trying to explain please leave me alone, I want to sleep, but my tongue is too clumsy, my aunt is saying, "You don't have a fever, Jenna, but your skin feels clammy cold and you're so thin! I hadn't realized . . ." and I'm trying to push them away, push their hands away, the man's voice is urgent, asking did I take something, did I take some drug, what did I take, please, Jenna, answer my question, but I'm floating now, floating/falling, I can't reach them to push their hands away, I can't scream at them to leave me alone, they are pleading with me to sit up, to wake up, someone is slapping my face, Jenna? Jenna? but I can't wake up, their voices are faint and fading like you'd hear on a cell phone dropped to the ground, somehow I am being pushed up, I am being made to stand, but my legs are gone, my legs are totally gone, I'd laugh this is so silly, but I guess I'm not strong enough to laugh, somebody is splashing cold water onto my face, but my face is frozen like with Novocain I can't feel my face, can't open my eyes, somebody is trying to push my arm through a sleeve, like a coat sleeve, the voices are loud and anxious and intrusive when I just want to sleep, and finally they go away, or anyway I can't hear them, sinking/falling/floating into inky-black emptiness like in a room that's dark and no windows and you sort of know that there must be furniture and things, has to be walls, ceiling, and a floor except you can't see them, for inside this room you are blind.

26.

i hate them. i will never forgive them. freaking like that like i'd OD'd on them. like if i'd wanted to kill myself, this is how i would do it: one downer! i am so totally mortified, everybody will know my so-called family called 911 to call an ambulance on christmas eve to have me carried out on a stretcher, taken to the ER to have my stomach pumped!!!

i guess this is what happened. it's not like i was there.

III

New Year

1

Soon as she's back from St. Bart's, Trina checks in.

"Baby, hey. I heard."

Her breath in my ear, almost I can feel it.

"You had, like, a bad trip? But you're okay now?"

I tell Trina yes. I'm more than okay.

I'm waiting for Trina to suggest that we get together, hang out. I can tell my aunt I'm going to the Yarrow Lake library downtown, I can walk. I've been missing Trina so. ". . . see, baby, I told you cut the pill in, like, quarters? Didn't I? Nobody would take all of it at once, baby."

I tell Trina I'm sorry, I must've got it wrong.

"Not from me you didn't get it wrong."

Trina pauses, breathing into the phone. I'm gripping my cell tight in my hand, I can feel my hand sweating.

Casually Trina asks, ". . . didn't tell anybody, baby, did you? Where you got the BZ from?" and I'm quick to say, "No.

Of course not, Trina." Sounding hurt that Trina would ask such a question, so she picks up on this. "Baby, I know. I know you wouldn't, you're like my closest friend. I'll call you tomorrow, baby. Maybe we can hang out."

After Trina's gone, my hand is still gripping the cell phone like my fingers need to be pried off.

2

Tell me about yourself, Jenna.

Tell me about your feelings.

Your thoughts. Your fears. Your dreams.

Smiling. Why is she smiling! Like a fishing line cast out so if I am weak and smile back, the hook will sink into me and Dr. Freer will haul me up like a big, squirmy fish.

I'm afraid of her. This woman. Afraid of how I hate her leathery skin, brown-pink lipstick, ribbed navy-blue turtle-neck, and gray flannel slacks. I hate the gold wedding band on her left hand, who cares? I hate her silly hoop earrings. I hate the framed diplomas on the wall behind her bookshelves, boasting. I hate her fleshy face creased into a smile, no matter, *I am not smiling back, am I? Hello?*

Afraid of so much hating! I know it's wrong, and it's stupid.

First session with Dr. Freer I wouldn't talk. Second session ended after twenty minutes. This is the third, it's going a little better. I don't feel so angry. My heart isn't beating so hard. As long as I can press the sharp edges of my fingernails against the inside of my arm where the skin is soft, I can concentrate on that.

Tell me your secrets, Jenna! I am the professional.

In the Yarrow Lake phone directory yellow pages, Dr. Freer has a small rectangular box to herself:

Freer, Meghan T., Ph.D.
N.H. Licensed Psychologist
Adolescents & Young Adults
Family Counseling

Pretending you are so wise. Placing framed photos in your office showing family scenes: the psychologist/mom with kids, a husband, skiing/sailing/hiking so your patients get the picture: NORMAL.

NORMAL can instruct. NORMAL can show how.

It's almost February. I've been back in school for three weeks. Fridays after school my aunt drives me to Dr. Freer's office in downtown Yarrow Lake. Four o'clock to four-fifty, a so-called hour that is fifty minutes.

Dr. Freer has met with my aunt and my uncle and knows the story.

As much as they know, anyway.

I am seeing Dr. Freer because of Christmas Eve. My "overdose"! Knocking me out instead of floating me through Christmas the way it was supposed to. How many times I have tried to explain, *I was not attempting suicide?*

It was a mistake I made. A stupid mistake. Trina and her friends must be laughing at me. Taking four times the dosage I was supposed to. Can't remember what I was thinking. My thoughts are confused. After my stomach was pumped, they told me the drug was Thorazine, a "psychotropic" used in the treatment of violent psychotics, I'd taken a dose strong enough to tranquilize a two-hundred-pound man.

Who gave me the drug? they asked. I said I didn't know his name, some guy at the mall. An "older" guy. I'd never seen him before and would never, never see him again.

Aunt Caroline and Uncle Dwight were so shocked! So sad, disappointed with me, I guess. Why I would do such a thing, why risk such harm to myself, why on Christmas Eve, why when they love me, oh Jenna *why?*

I'm ashamed, I don't know *why.*

It was a stupid mistake, not a "suicide attempt," truly! I wish my aunt and my uncle believed me. It's like Mom not believing me.

I am not "suicidal." I am not "depressed."

I am not "using" drugs, that was one time only.

This session with Dr. Freer, maybe it will be the last.

If I impress Dr. Freer that I am NORMAL. Like her.

". . . kind of embarrassed, actually."

"Embarrassed, Jenna? Why?"

"Because at school people know about it. Some of them. I guess my teachers know. I'm embarrassed that people think I tried . . . tried to hurt myself . . . but it was an accident, and accidents are stupid."

"'Accidents are stupid,' Jenna? Can you talk to me a little about that?"

No! No, I can't.

". . . the opposite of, like, a conscious decision. A conscious act. Something that's an accident can come to seem like it's you in some way, in other people's minds, but actually it isn't, it isn't you. It's just . . ."

"An accidental overdose of a potentially lethal drug, Jenna, on Christmas Eve, in circumstances like yours, you suggest isn't in some legitimate way representative of you? Is that what you are suggesting, dear?"

Dear. It's to work the fishhook into my mouth, so Dr. Freer can haul me ashore. My face shuts tight, my gaze turns stony, so Dr. Freer gets the signal.

After my stomach was pumped, they asked me about drugs at the high school, how available are drugs in Yarrow Lake, what kinds of drugs are teenagers taking. Even a woman detective, pretending to be sympathetic.

As if I would rat on my friends! My closest friend, Trina.

"Talk to me, Jenna. What are your associations with *accident, accidental?*"

Dr. Freer has a way of leaning forward, clasping her long leathery fingers together, fixing me with her eyes that are a startling pale blue. A way of prying that scares me, I feel close to giving in.

No! I can't.

Can't talk about it with you. Not with anyone.

This is one thing I like about the psychologist's office: She has hanging plants in the windows, spiky leaves and tiny white flowers, and on the walls poster-size photographs of a lake with sailboats (Yarrow Lake?) and mountains that are much larger than the White Mountains, with steep snowy slopes, dazzling white peaks. The sky is so blue in these photos. Like windows I can look into, to escape *in the blue*, not trapped in this office, being dissected like some pathetic beetle.

Trina says never tell them what you feel, only what they want you to feel. That's what NORMAL is: what adults want you to feel.

Dr. Freer is asking if I have "close friends" at my new school, which is a question she has asked before. To be NORMAL, you have to have "close friends." I'm vague in answering: Yes. No. Maybe. I don't know what Aunt Caroline has told Dr. Freer about Trina.

Trina is my friend. My friend I can't trust.

I love Trina.

Dr. Freer asks if I have remained in touch with my friends in Tarrytown. Vaguely I murmur yes, but actually I never answer their e-mails or calls, mostly they've stopped trying to contact me. It's too much effort.

I hate people feeling sorry for me. I don't feel sorry for myself!

Dr. Freer keeps poking, prodding. Asking now about my teachers, classes, grades. So boring!

"Jenna? I can't hear you—will you speak more clearly? And will you look at me, dear? Thank you!"

Like this is kindergarten. Like I am so totally screwed up.

I tell Dr. Freer what she wants to hear, that I like my teachers okay, my classes are okay, my fall term grades were better than I expected. (At least I didn't flunk a single course. I know, the McCartys are disappointed in me. Aunt Caroline is thinking how disappointed Mom would be if she knew.) I hear myself tell Dr. Freer that this semester I might join the school newspaper staff, I might try out for girls' chorus, if my running time improves I might try out for the girls' track team.

Dr. Freer beams at all this good news. Nothing impresses an adult like hearing of your "activities" at school.

"You were on the track team at your previous school, weren't you?"

You tell me, Doctor. You have my records.

Dr. Freer asks about my physical health. Have my injuries healed? Do I suffer from headaches? Often people who've had concussions are susceptible to headaches, which can lead to an attempt to "self-medicate" by taking unauthorized drugs. . . .

In the blue you can fall, and fall. I'm staring at the blue sky like enamel in one of the poster-size photos of maybe the Rocky Mountains. Thousands of miles away.

Dr. Freer is always circling around drugs. It occurs to me,

maybe she's making a tape of these sessions. Maybe there's a surveillance camera in the ceiling. A psychologist who works with adolescents in Yarrow Lake might inform to the Yarrow Lake cops.

Next, Dr. Freer asks about boys.

Clearing her throat in a way to suggest the subject isn't "boys" but "sex."

None of your business! I don't share secrets with nosy strangers.

Dr. Freer flashes the fishhook smile, but her eyes are uneasy.

On a bookshelf is what looks like a spherical glass paperweight with a miniature mountain inside that's made of some glittery mineral and a blue sky over the mountain that's magnified by the glass so that it seems to shimmer. It's so beautiful, *in the blue* inside a glass ball.

Psychologists have to ask about sex, for sure. Like sex is all there is, no matter what people pretend.

Damn if I will tell Dr. Freer that I don't see any guys, except when I'm with Trina and her friends. That I am in love with a boy named Gabriel Saint-Croix, who doesn't know I exist except as somebody to feel sorry for.

Crippled people and losers. Crow has such a thing for.

Mom used to ask me about boys too. I told her lots of things but kept back a lot more. Mom wasn't prying, I guess, just wanting me to be popular and have friends but not too popular and not the wrong kind of friends.

I wonder what Mom would think of Crow! She'd be stunned.

Near the end of the session, Dr. Freer asks about "dreams," "memories." For sure, she wants to ask about Mom. What happened on the Tappan Zee Bridge. She knows, just wants me to tell her. Whatever answer I give, I'm not looking at her; my voice is a low resentful murmur.

I miss my mom, okay? Like every minute, every hour, and every day, but it's no big deal, I can cope.

Asks about my father. I tell her my relationship with my father is "zero."

"Jenna, of course you and your father have a relationship. You must know your father is helping to pay for your sessions with me? That has been explained to you, I think?"

No. Hasn't been explained to me.

". . . talk to me about why you are so hostile to your father? Even to the idea of his helping to pay for your therapy? Don't you think that it's natural for a father to wish to help in such a way?"

I'm on my feet, asking to use Dr. Freer's bathroom, please. I've used it before. Don't have to be told where it is.

In the bathroom I examine the soft white flesh on the inside of my left elbow that's stippled red from my fingernails digging in. Some of the tiny wounds are older and healing, the new ones are bleeding thinly. I'm surprised, my arm throbs and hurts. In Dr. Freer's office my arm felt numb like the rest of me.

Tell me what you feel, Jenna.

Smiling at my face in the mirror. There's a rosy light in here, the psychologist's patients see the least ugly of their faces. I like it, my arm throbbing! The tiny bleeding wounds are some kind of weird relief.

Nobody can see. Nobody knows. It's no big deal. I keep my sleeves pulled down past my wrists like a junkie.

Then, this happens. Weird!

When I return from the bathroom, Dr. Freer is searching for a book on one of the shelves, her back to me. I'm quick and quiet, and my fingers close over the glass paperweight that's just the right size to fit in my hand, a little heavier than I expected, but already it's been transferred to my backpack, on the floor beside the chair I've been sitting in.

I can see Trina smiling, impressed. Baby, you are so *cool*.

I am, I think. I'm learning.

I wish Dr. Freer caught on that I don't like her. Really I don't like her. I'm not even listening to her. That phony smile, showing her gums. Hoop earrings, ridiculous. She's too old. That smudgy brown-pink lipstick, which isn't exactly glamorous. Mom wore it sometimes, it looked okay on her.

Dr. Freer has a book to lend me. "If you like it, Jenna, of course you should keep it."

The Member of the Wedding by Carson McCullers. I've read this novel, it was a favorite of Mom's. I'm blushing and stammering, telling Dr. Freer I've already read it, it's a beautiful novel, I guess, but so sad, and Dr. Freer lays her hand on my arm, saying she first read *The Member of the Wedding* when she was twelve, and has many times since. "It's a novel about loss, growing up with loss, and growing beyond loss."

On her feet, Dr. Freer isn't as tall as I am. Like Mom, the last year or so. It makes me uneasy, being taller than grown women. Makes me resent them, I don't know why.

Each time our session ends, Dr. Freer walks with me to the door. Shakes my hand, smiles. Her gums show, she's smiling so. Up close her skin doesn't look so leathery—I guess it's just tan from being outdoors. Her eyes are such an amazing blue.

The way Dr. Freer is talking to me, laying her hand on my arm like that, it comes over me like a wave of icy water: *She wants me to like her!* I'm afraid of this thought. Like hearing Aunt Caroline's muffled sobs in her bedroom one afternoon and knowing it's my fault, she's crying because of me.

I don't mean to hurt you. It's just, I'm a scorpion. What do you expect?

3

Why I took Dr. Freer's paperweight I don't know.

It's so beautiful, maybe that's why. It's to punish Dr. Freer, maybe that's why. To punish myself maybe.

I have to keep the paperweight a secret from Aunt Caroline. I will have to hide it in my room.

If Mom knew, she'd be dismayed. The person I am now, Mom would not wish to know.

Jenna, this isn't like you. Jenna, what is happening?

Won't even show Trina. Can't trust Trina, she'd tease me sometime in front of other people. She'd want to see the paperweight, hold it in her hand.

In my room at night when I can't sleep, I can stare at the glass sphere with the mountain inside. I've positioned it on my desk with a light behind it to make it glow. The miniature mountain is made of some bluish-gray mineral. The sky is deep-blue curved glass. When you shake the paperweight, flakes of "snow" drift over everything as in a dream.

I wonder if it's expensive. If Dr. Freer will notice it's missing and know that I am the thief.

I'm so ashamed! This is the first thing I've stolen from anybody known to me. The first of any value. Uncle Dwight's Oxys don't count—he didn't even know he still had them. I don't know why I took it, and I don't know what I will do with it now.

4

Typed in *SUICIDE* on the Internet, and man!—there's like a million hits. Clicked onto some Christian Youth Forum. A message came up:

> In America in these troubled times a young person aged 14–26 commits suicide every 13 minutes.

There's a discussion group. You can type in your response. I type:

> In the Country of the Blue
> there is no you
> THAT'S WHY

5

In March, this happens.

Like nothing I could imagine. Not ever.

I'm due to meet up with my aunt in about an hour at her favorite coffee shop in downtown Yarrow Lake. I'm in a neighborhood of small storefront shops on South Main Street. Staring into the crowded display window of Saint-Croix Carpenter & Cabinetmaker. Most of what I see is furniture. Except for a dim light at the rear, the store doesn't look open.

It's a Friday after school. I am supposed to be in Dr. Freer's office. Last week, I canceled. This week, I just didn't go in.

Waited in the vestibule of the office building for Aunt Caroline to drive away. Then I ran out.

Can't. Won't. Nobody can make me.

This cold, fresh air! Deep in my lungs, clearing my head. It's a pure kind of high. I'm feeling excited and out of breath;

I ran like a half mile. It's a bright, sunny winter afternoon, a few days after a heavy snowfall, so streets and sidewalks are mostly cleared, but there are banks and heaps of snow blinding in the sunshine. Like the world is meant to be white, glaring-white. I'm shading my eyes, peering inside this shop that's between a shoe repair and a hardware store with a big red banner GOING OUT OF BUSINESS EVERYTHING HALF PRICE.

In the front window is a beautiful carved old table with curved legs. Also a glass breakfront of some beautiful stained wood. If I had the nerve, I'd try the door, go inside. Pretend to be a customer. I could say that my aunt had some special old antique that needed to be repaired or restored.

I could say, *I am a friend of Crow's!*

In fact I have not spoken with Crow since the second day of school. I have tried not to look for him. Once in the school library during study period I turned a corner, saw Crow seated at a computer like any other guy, frowning at the screen. His black hair was stiff-spiky, and he was wearing a long-sleeved T-shirt and a leather vest studded with inverted Vs and stained jeans and biker boots. A girl was with him, chewing gum. A red-haired girl whose name is something like Flax, one of Trina's rivals she totally hates, she's nudging her thigh against Crow's arm, slipping her hand inside his shirt, and Crow pushes her hand away and continues with the computer like almost she isn't there.

I escaped before Crow glanced up. Not that Crow was aware of me in the slightest.

"I wish."

What do I wish? I don't know. My brain feels like broken glass is being shaken inside it. I can't even think of Dr. Freer waiting for me, and I don't show up, and it's the second week I don't show up, so she'll call my aunt, she's concerned, she's wondering where I am, where the girl who'd OD'd on Thorazine on Christmas Eve has run away to, the thief who stole her beautiful glass paperweight when her back was turned.

I tried to explain to my aunt and my uncle I didn't want to return to Dr. Freer. But they were upset, saying they thought I'd been making progress. Saying I had promised, hadn't I?

I guess. Maybe.

Jenna, this isn't like you. Jenna, what is happening?

I promised them, after my stomach was pumped, I would never try any drug again, never, never again. Since classes started in January, and I've been hanging out with Trina and her friends, I haven't exactly kept that promise.

I won't make any stupid mistake ever again. Never wind up

in the ER with a tube down my throat like a boa constrictor sucking out the contents of my stomach, never, never again.

I'm remembering how I bicycled out to where Crow's family lives on Deer Isle Road. Especially when I feel lonely, I think of this. I haven't been back since, but I remember the ramshackle farmhouse at the end of the rutted lane and the swaybacked gray horse and the shaggy black goat in the front pasture *baaa*ing at me. Hilly countryside that people like Ryan Moeller call trailer-trash territory.

Nobody seems to be inside Saint-Croix Carpenter & Cabinetmaker. A few pedestrians pass behind me on the sidewalk, but no one stops. Sometimes a reflection looms up behind my reflection in the front window, but it's no one, nothing. I think, *This is not a movie or TV, only boring life, where nothing happens.*

I'm halfway up the block in the direction of the coffee shop when I see a man in a motorized wheelchair approaching on the icy sidewalk, having some trouble with the chair. He's a beefy, heavyset middle-aged man with a scruffy beard and black hair streaked with white that's thin at the crown of his head but pulled back into a straggly ponytail. It's so weird—you see half-bald guys with ponytails and you'd think their wives or kids would tell them how they look. This man in the wheelchair is wearing a soiled Windbreaker and work pants, and his breath is steaming, he's angry about something. The wheelchair is lurching and skidding. He's cursing in some foreign language. I'm hesitant to ask if he needs help, not just because this man's face is flushed but because you are supposed to be very tactful with handicapped people, not to hurt their pride.

The ponytail man glares at me. Like he knows I am debating whether to speak to him, to risk making him angrier. "Goddamn thing is always breaking down—is it stuck? What's stuck? Is something caught in the wheel?"

There's a chunk of ice caught in the spokes of the left rear wheel. I manage to work it loose as the ponytail man curses and fumes in heavily accented English. "*Mademoiselle, merci!* You are a *très belle jeune fille, très capable.*" He reaches out to shake my hand or just to grab it. He's wearing black leather fingerless gloves like bikers wear. Laughing and baring ruined teeth, and giving off a strong odor of whiskey.

Still, the wheelchair is skidding on wavy patches of ice. I volunteer to push the ponytail man along the sidewalk. Where a moment before he was angry, now he's genial and even charming. Asking where I am from, I don't sound like New Hampshire.

"I—I'm not from here. I just live here."

"'Not from here. Just live here.' *Moi aussi!*"

The ponytail man laughs as if I've said something witty. I can see that even with his flushed coarse skin and the ponytail straggling down his muscular back, he's a good-looking man, accustomed to female attention.

A wheelchair is heavy to push! In just half a block my arms are beginning to ache.

"Here we are, mademoiselle! *Merci beaucoup*—you are so kind."

The doorway of Saint-Croix Carpenter & Cabinetmaker.

Crow's father? The ponytail man? He must be.

Roland Saint-Croix! Must be.

And there suddenly is Crow himself crossing the street in our direction. Crow, in leather jacket, jeans, biker boots. Bareheaded and his spiky hair disheveled in the wind. On his shoulders is a toddler bundled up in a snowsuit, squealing with pleasure at the bouncy piggyback ride. Crow, seeing me, the look on my face, laughs.

"Jenna, is it? Hello."

I am stricken with embarrassment. I can feel heat rising in my face and can only stammer hello.

He knows. Must know. Why I am here.

The ponytail man is saying in a jovial voice, "You know my son Gabriel, you go to the same school, eh?" and Crow says quickly, seeing how uncomfortable I am, "Jenna isn't in my class, Papa. She's younger," and the ponytail man says, winking at me, "But of course the girl is younger! And pretty too, I can see that."

Crow introduces me to his father, Roland Saint-Croix, and to *le petit Roland*, who ignores me, squealing and kicking as he's swung down into Mr. Saint-Croix's brawny arms. He's a beautiful child and obviously spoiled. I've never heard such shrieks. Passersby on the sidewalk glance at us, bemused. (Could they think we all belong to the same noisy family?) Except that little Roland has fine taffy-colored hair instead of jet-black hair, and he's lighter skinned than Crow and Mr. Saint-Croix. Still, the family resemblance among the three is almost comical: deep-set eyes, longish nose, strong chin.

Crow says, an edge of exasperation in his voice, "You want him, Papa? Take him inside, it's cold out here."

Crow and his father exchange remarks in French, which I can't follow. Crow laughs, blushing; Mr. Saint-Croix sniggers, with a glance at me. I guess it must be some sort of sexual innuendo. Like, Roland Saint-Croix is in a wheelchair, still, he's the father of this young child? That's the joke?

Crow says, "C'mon inside, Jenna, for a few minutes and get warm. See what Saint-Croix *père et fils* do for a living."

Père et fils: father and son.

I love the way Crow says this. The pride in his voice.

I try to explain that I have to meet my aunt, but somehow, I don't know how, I'm inside the cabinetmaker's shop with the Saint-Croixes, a bell attached to the door jangles overhead. After the snow-bright sunshine I'm stumbling into things. Crow takes my arm to guide me. "This is—what's it called?— a maze. You could get lost."

So many things! The interior of Mr. Saint-Croix's shop is nearly as crowded as the display window. Everywhere, some stacked on top of one another, are tables, chairs, bureaus. There's a passageway, just wide enough for Mr. Saint-Croix's wheelchair, that leads to the rear of the shop, where a radio is playing French pop music. Here are open floor space, work-tables, a massive cluttered desk, a tattered easy chair, a hot plate and a coffeemaker, and scattered, very dirty carpets. Little Roland's toys are underfoot. There's a strong smell of coffee, varnish, and wood polish. Crow takes me farther to the rear to show me a dining room table he's restoring: "First I removed the gummy old polish, then I sanded the wood, which is cherrywood—very nice, see?—next I will be staining it. This is a table from maybe 1870, Papa says. The owners didn't take good care of it. See these carvings? Gummed up with dirt. People don't know the things that exist under their noses."

Mr. Saint-Croix—who has wheeled himself briskly to his desk, where he clears a space to set little Roland—calls over contemptuously, "The Americans, not all but most, excuse me, mademoiselle, they are *cochons*."

Cochons. I've never heard this word before, but somehow I know what it means. "Pigs?"

Mr. Saint-Croix is delighted. Crow laughs. Somehow, Jenna knows a little French.

This visit! With Crow and his father! Like the most wonderful dream you can recall afterward only in fragments.

Crow shows me around the shop as if it's the most fascinating place in the world. (I guess it is. I'm staring at everything I see.) Crow explains the kind of work his father does, what he has learned from him, and how much he has yet to learn. It's so strange to hear any guy talking about his father like this. Stranger too to see any adult's actual work that can be touched. (I don't even know what my father does, I guess. Makes money?) There's both pride and exasperation in

Crow's voice. The way he glances over at his father, who's talking loudly and laughing on the phone, I can see that Crow loves his father, but. "Thanks for being nice to Papa, Jenna. He's a wild guy, eh?"

"He seems very . . ."

"Like I told you, he was in Vietnam, came back with some medals, which he threw away. He won't talk about it. Not even with me. He's kind of hard to live with mostly. He likes you; he's on his good behavior with you."

Little Roland has been devouring a jelly doughnut and has made quite a mess. Mr. Saint-Croix hasn't been watching him, so Crow goes over to wipe the child's face with a wetted tissue. It's strange to see a guy like Crow who looks like a biker—is a biker—so patient with a small child. So tender. It's like Crow is from some other world, not the suburban world I know. In Tarrytown, he'd stand out. The way, when Crow smiles, you can see that his teeth aren't the smooth white even teeth you expect.

I'm thinking that Crow loves his little brother, a half brother? I want to confide in him that I have a stepbrother. I've met Porter only once. I don't know him, don't love him, though.

As if he can read my thoughts, Crow asks about my father. I tell him that my father is a businessman—"successful," I guess—remarried and living in California in an expensive new house. We don't see each other very much.

"Why's that?"

"He left us."

"'Us'—like your mother and you?"

Why are you asking me these things? Making me want to cry.

Crow says, frowning, "You don't want to lose contact with your father, Jenna. He is your father."

"But—I don't like him."

The way I say this, both Crow and I start laughing. It sounds so comical somehow.

"'Like,' 'don't like'—still, he's your father. That won't change." Crow is watching Mr. Saint-Croix as the red-faced man paws through papers on his desk looking for—what? A stump of a cigar, half smoked. Though little Roland is playing close by, Crow's father doesn't hesitate to light up. "Like, with my mom too. Last we heard from her, a few years ago, she sent a crate of citrus fruit for Christmas—grapefruit, oranges, lemons. Just a card saying Merry Christmas." Crow laughs, ruefully.

Suddenly the bell above the front door jangles, and someone comes in briskly. Not a customer, the way she's clattering in our direction. A glamorous girl in stiletto-heel boots, faux-leopard jacket, and skintight shiny leather trousers, her fleshy face heavily made up and her strawberry-blond hair floating in frizzy waves. She's noisy and exclamatory, greeting Mr. Saint-Croix and little Roland, stooping to kiss the man's veiny red cheek and to lift the squealing child in her hands. Her nails are as dazzling as talons: at least two inches long, filed blunt at the ends, the color of frost. Little Roland screams, *Mama!* and the girl coos, nuzzles, and scolds him. Finally she notices Crow on the other side of the room, and me beside him, and stares at us for a weird rude moment without speaking.

Crow is going to introduce us, but the girl addresses him in a sharp teasing voice as if I'm not here: *"Eh, Gabriel! C'est qui ça, ta petite amie avec les yeux adorants?"* and Crow mutters, *"Qu'est-ce que ça peut te faire?"* Impossible to tell if Crow is angry, hurt, or embarrassed, his face has tightened like a mask. Seeing that she has succeeded in upsetting him, the girl in the leopard-skin coat turns her back to us, nuzzling little Roland, who has closed a small, jelly-stained fist in her hair.

I'm thinking that this glamorous girl must be Crow's older sister. Obviously, little Roland is hers. Now I remember Trina saying that Crow's sister brought a baby home and that Crow was helping out with the family.

Crow says, "Claudette? I'm going now."

Without glancing over her shoulder, the girl says, "So? Go."

Mr. Saint-Croix calls over something to Crow, in his heavily accented English that's almost indistinguishable from French. Whatever is going on in the family, what the under-currents of emotion are, no outsider could decode. Claudette and Mr. Saint-Croix are chattering in French and laughing in a way that makes me uncomfortable. Are they talking about me? If so, it's to annoy Crow, who's scowling and flush faced. There's bluish smoke wafting about Mr. Saint-Croix, but Claudette doesn't seem to mind. In fact, even with little Roland clambering about her feet, she's lighting up a parchment-colored cigarette and exhaling smoke of her own.

Crow says, "C'mon, Jenna. I'll drive you."

It's past five P.M. Aunt Caroline will be waiting for me in the coffee shop. By now she might know that I skipped my session with Dr. Freer. If she doesn't, I guess I will have to tell her.

For a dazed moment I think that I will be riding on the back of Crow's Harley-Davidson, roaring along the Main Street of Yarrow Lake in the cold, gusty air. But it's a battered minivan behind the shop, with SAINT-CROIX CARPENTER & CABINETMAKER painted in red on its sides. I have to haul myself up into the cab, it's so high from the ground. The interior of the van is freezing and smells of stale cigar smoke and varnish. The passenger seat is ripped, and the windshield is finely cracked. So strange, and so wonderful, to be alone with Crow like this: like a couple. Our breaths are steaming in the cold air.

Stained rags, styrofoam cups, empty beer cans, and cigar butts are strewn on the minivan floor. I want to laugh, it's like riding in a mobile junkyard.

Crow asks where to? and I tell him, the coffee shop/bakery on Mount Street. I'm so happy to be here, in this smelly, rattling minivan, I don't want the ride to ever end. I'm too shy to look at Crow except out of the corner of my eye. But I can see his hands gripping the steering wheel: big knuckles, long fingers, dirt-edged nails. I can feel him close beside me. I'm thinking, *If Trina saw me now!* My best friend would never forgive me.

I wish I could call Crow by his true name: Gabriel. The name he's called by his family.

Since Claudette came bursting into the shop, Crow has been acting different. He's edgy, irritated. Not at me. I guess he must be brooding over his sister, who was so rude to us, and his father, who's been drinking, and little Roland—his nephew?—and maybe he's also thinking of his mother, who left (when? why?). I would love to ask Crow about his mother sometime.

If we see each other again. If we are ever alone like this again.

Crow gives me a sidelong glance. Like he's checking me out.

"This van is something, eh? Not what you're used to."

"It's . . . very high."

"Yeah, you look down on other drivers. Some drivers. Mostly, driving a van, people look down on you."

I'm not sure how to interpret this. Close up, I can see nicks and scars in Crow's face. I remember he said he's been in a wreck too. (Maybe more than one?) I wonder if, driving, he thinks of the danger. If there is something scary, and exciting, about driving after you have been in a wreck, and lived.

Crow is a good driver, for sure. The van has a stick shift, which he handles with authority. Next year I will take driver's ed at school. I mean, it's required. They don't teach you stick, though. The thought of driving a car makes me feel excited, sickish.

In a car you can lose control. The weight of the car will propel you forward. Helpless.

Crow says, "It's been a while since I've seen you, Jenna. I heard you almost OD'd at Christmas."

This is a shock! I don't know what to say.

I hear myself stammer it was a really stupid mistake . . .

"The mistake is hanging out with Trina Holland."

"But Trina is my . . ."

The minivan is lumbering along Main Street. Crow is an aggressive driver but can't make much headway in this traffic. I am so surprised at what he's said. That Crow has any thoughts at all about me. "Trina is, like, my closest friend. I thought you and Trina—"

Crow laughs. Runs his fingers through his hair so it looks fierce and spiky, like the feathers of a savage bird. Meaning— what? He and Trina are broken up? Or never were a couple? Or Crow can handle Trina, Trina and her friends are no danger to *him*?

I'm kind of stunned. For a long time I've been thinking that Crow would be impressed that Trina Holland has time for me. Trina Holland likes *me*! And aren't Trina's friends, the guys she hangs out with, mostly Crow's friends too?

Maybe something happened between them that I don't know about.

"It wasn't Trina's fault, Crow. It was mine."

Crow shrugs like *okay*. Whatever I want to think.

"Jax gave me the pill. You know, Jax Yardman . . ."

Sure. What*ever*.

"I made a mistake; I was feeling kind of bad. I guess I wanted to sleep right through Christmas. Just, like, *out*."

"Why?"

"Why—what?"

"Why'd you feel bad?"

This is the question everybody tries to ask me. Aunt Caroline, Uncle Dwight, Dr. Freer. But nobody has asked it blunt and in your face like Crow.

"Because I miss my mother. Maybe you know—my mother and I were in a car crash last May. That's why I'm here in Yarrow Lake. I live with my aunt now."

"I heard, yeah. I'm sorry, Jenna."

Damn if I am going to cry. The way Crow says *sorry*.

This frayed old safety belt I buckled myself into, I'm glad that it's holding me tight now. I can feel myself straining against it, like something is trying to throw me forward to hurt me.

Crow asks me what happened, and I tell him: It was a head-on collision, on the Tappan Zee Bridge. My mother lost control of her car. She veered into another lane, hit a truck. She and the other driver died. I was pretty banged up, but I survived. It was thought that the setting sun blinded my mother so she couldn't see, and everything happened so quickly. . . .

"The Tappan Zee is such a big bridge, did you know, Gabriel?

It's three miles long. I dream about it all the time. The Hudson River is really wide at that point; like a nightmare, it just goes on and on. . . ." I'm out of breath, words are rushing from me. After a pause I hear myself say, "I caused the crash, I think."

"How?"

Crow is so quick and matter-of-fact. Right away asking me *how*, like he isn't judging me or trying to convince me I must be wrong.

"I pulled at the wheel. I panicked, I guess. There was something on the bridge in front of us—I couldn't see exactly, the sun was blinding . . ."

My voice trails off. I can't believe that I have told Crow this, which I have never told any other person.

"What was it, Jenna, you thought you saw?"

"A deer, maybe. A dog . . ."

I'm waiting for Crow to ask the obvious question: Was anything found on the bridge in the wreck? A deer, a dog?

I'm waiting for Crow to ask: Have you told anybody? Have you confessed that you caused an accident that killed two innocent people?

But Crow says only, shaking his head, "That's heavy. For you to keep to yourself. Man!"

Later I will realize that I called Crow Gabriel, and it was so natural-sounding, neither of us noticed at the time. At least I think Crow didn't notice.

"So anything that happens to Jenna, that's hurtful and punishing, it's what she deserves."

Crow says this like stating a fact. Not trying to argue me out of it.

I'm not crying, but my nose is running; I'm wiping it on the edge of my hand like a little kid. Crow pulls a crumpled tissue out of his pocket and hands it to me without comment. He's used to wiping little Roland's nose, I guess.

"Jesus! I know what it's like, Jenna. Accident-prone."

He has turned onto Mount Street, where traffic is tight. Up the block is Elvira's Coffee & Bakery, with a gingerbread man sign that creaks in the wind. It's strange to me like a dream to be here high in the cab of an unfamiliar vehicle staring out at shops and storefronts that look transformed. "I can get out here, Gabriel. Thank you."

I don't want Aunt Caroline to see me with Crow. To see me getting out of this van. There would be too much to explain.

Crow brakes the van to a stop. Leans across me to open the door, which is heavy and sticks. Crow is so close, I can feel his breath on my skin. His jacket sleeve has pushed up—I see the tail of the coiled green snake just above his wrist. Crow was close to Trina once, wasn't he? Here is proof.

"Take care, *chérie*, it's a big step to the street."

On the sidewalk I watch the minivan move away. Within seconds it becomes one of several vans and small trucks on Mount Street. He called me *chérie*!

6

march 11, 2005

dear dad,

thank you for the christmas gifts.
i am sorry not to call back.
i dont do much e-mail here. its not like tarrytown.
my friends in yarrow lake arent into it.
i am happy here. thank you for inviting me to visit.
i am busy now with classes. maybe sometime.

jenna

(It took me forty minutes to write this. Trying to decide if I had
to say "love, Jenna." In his cards and e-mails to me Dad always
says "love, Dad." It's so phony, though. I hate it. I just can't say
"love" to him. Not anymore.)

7

"I wish."

At school I try not to look for Crow. Try not to stare past the others' faces hoping to see his. Try not to hang out at the back of the school. Try not to drift through the seniors' wing, where a sophomore is out of place.

I was so surprised: Trina knew! Only a few hours after Crow left me off on Mount Street, I'm in my room at home and my cell rings, and Trina's voice is reedy and sharp in my ear. "Hey baby, heard you hooked up with Crow." I stammered telling her he'd given me a ride, that was all. Trina laughed to show this was cool with her, why'd she care if Crow gave me a ride home. I said, Crow didn't give me a ride home, just a ride from one part of downtown to another. Trina laughed and clicked off. Yet next day at school, in the cafeteria, Trina sinks her nails into my wrist, says, "So where's Crow? Why're you with us, where's Crow?" like she's angry and sneering but smiling at me, leaning close almost like she's kissing me. And Kiki, and Dolores, and T-Man, and Rust, and Roger, and Jax are looking on.

"Trina, Crow just gave me a ride. A few blocks. He saw me walking, it was cold . . ."

"In his dad's truck, eh? That must've been warm."

Trina's sitting between T-Man and Dolores, and there's no room for me at their end of the table. I'm standing with my tray, beginning to feel anxious. (Maybe Trina is teasing? Trina is always teasing!) "Jenna, hey. Here's a place." Rust Haber pulls out a chair for me next to him, but I don't want to sit with Rust. He's a short, blunt-faced boy with muscled arms and shoulders from working out and a smirky smile, and Trina has told me Rust is "kind of into" me—thinks I'm "cute"—but his eyes on me are never friendly, always kind of taunting. Like, if I give in and sit by him, if I ever hook up with him, he'll laugh at me afterward.

There's Jax Yardman. I don't trust him either. There's Kiki Weaver, pulling out a chair for me. "Jenna? C'mon." I'm sitting next to Kiki, staring at the food on my plate. At the other end of the noisy table Trina is laughing, I don't dare look at her. Kiki is a big-boned girl with long, straight no-color hair streaked with purple. Every time I see Kiki, she has added another silver pin to her face, so she's glittering like a pin-cushion. Kiki has a big chest, not like Trina, who's size zero. Kiki leans close to me, saying, "Trina's pissed at you, but she'll get over it if you act like you're sorry."

"Crow only just gave me a ride in his—"

"Sure. Trina knows."

". . . it was just, like, he felt sorry for me, I guess. He . . ."

Kiki makes a gesture like to signal this is an obvious fact, everybody knows. Why'd I think I should explain?

8.

Chérie he called me. When he leaned across me to open the door of the van. Remembering that, I felt dazed, dizzy. I wanted to cry, to laugh, to scream. I wanted to kiss his mouth, which was so close to mine.

Chérie he called me. *Take care*, chérie, *it's a big step to the street.*

The pronunciation is *shay-ree*. Meaning *dear, dear one*.

In my French dictionary it also means *beloved, precious*.

In March, I've begun auditing French II.

First they told me no, it couldn't be allowed. If I wanted to take French II, I should have enrolled back in September.

"But I didn't want to take it then, Mr. Goddard. I want to take it now."

I got excited, I guess. Just felt so frustrated!

Finally Mr. Goddard said okay. As long as my study period was at the same time French II was taught. *Highly irregular. No academic credit.* I told Mr. Goddard I didn't care about academic credit, I just wanted to learn French.

Mr. Goddard adjusted his glasses on his nose and gave me a look like I am so totally, terminally weird it's impossible to communicate with me. "Jenna, this is a public high school. What if everyone just wanted to 'learn' and didn't want 'academic credit'?"

It's a small class anyway, only fourteen students. Mrs. Laport—Madame Laport, we call her—seems pleased that weird as I am, I've come along to take another seat. (Most students at Yarrow High take Spanish if they take any foreign language at all.) She smiles at me like she can't figure me out. I'm doing the homework, taking quizzes and tests, and really seem to enjoy the conversation exercises, which are the last fifteen minutes of each class. My grades, not "official" but just for me, are mostly As. Madame Laport says, "Jenna, *vous vous êtes beaucoup appliquée, pourquoi?*" and I tell her, enunciating each word with care like a toddler taking baby steps, "*Parce que le français est une langue très belle.*"

9

I am so *ashamed*.

I am so *angry*.

Dazed, like. Almost I don't know if I am standing or sit-ting—sitting, I guess. Later it will seem to me unreal as a dream where things are sliding and skidding and you can't catch your breath to figure out where you are, or why.

My uncle Dwight McCarty is asking why, why did I take the glass paperweight from Dr. Freer's office. "Was it to hurt us, Jenna? Or yourself?" and I can't answer.

Uncle Dwight and I are in his office study, which is at the rear of the house, a large rectangular room with mostly glass walls and a glass skylight. This is not a room I have ever entered by myself and only rarely with anyone else. It is not a room in which I would be welcome, as my little cousins Becky and Mikey would not be welcome. It's a little scary. Uncle Dwight has shut the door.

I guess he and my aunt Caroline decided that next time there was a problem with her niece, he would speak with me first. Because always it has been Aunt Caroline until now. And now it's just Uncle Dwight speaking in his calm, clench-jawed way like a reasonable man who is *trying to understand*, oh, man, he is *trying very hard to understand* why anyone would steal from someone who wants to help her, but, like, he *can't understand*.

". . . Jenna? To hurt us, your aunt and me, or . . ."

The incriminating evidence, the glass paperweight with the glittery mineral mountain and swath of pure-blue sky, is on my uncle's desk. I can't look at anything else.

" . . . must have realized, Jenna, that Dr. Freer would notice, and know that the person who took it had to be . . ."

Did I? Or didn't I care? I can't remember.

Poor Uncle Dwight! He's perspiring and breathing hard like a man trudging uphill, wondering where he's going. I wish that I could shrink into a tiny wisp of something like milkweed seed that could blow away and disappear. Earlier today at school I was feeling kind of good about myself. Gym class went pretty well (basketball, where I'm an okay player and Dara Bowen is always encouraging us), and I got a B– on my paper for history ("Child Labor in the First American

Textile Mill, 1790"), so coming home to this, to my uncle frowning and clenching his jaw, and Aunt Caroline hiding away, not wanting to see me, is a shock. There's a buzzing in my ears that's the pressure of blood, I remember from when I was in the hospital. I want to tell my uncle, *My head isn't right, my thoughts are confused, it was the blue sky I wanted.*

Instead I hear my voice, mumbling and sullen, saying, "I don't know. I don't know why I took it." My nose is running, I'm wiping it with the edge of my hand the way my eight-year-old cousin Mikey is scolded for doing.

"'Don't know,' Jenna? What do you mean?"

I mean what I said! I don't know.

My poor uncle is staring at me blank faced. It's funny how you never really look at some people, especially older relatives. To be somebody's uncle must be, like, the biggest bore, even worse than being somebody's aunt. *You aren't really my uncle,* I'm thinking. *It's just Aunt Caroline who is my aunt.*

If I'd known what was waiting for me in this house, I would've stayed away. Could not have faced them. So ashamed, they found Dr. Freer's paperweight in my desk! (I wasn't trying very hard to hide it. Every night I've taken it out to hold in my hand. It's been several weeks now, I'd begun to think Dr. Freer would not notice it was gone.) It makes me angry to think of Aunt Caroline going into my room and poking in my things. Not just my desk but my bureau drawers, my closet. I have a journal I write in sometimes, but it's always in my backpack, and my backpack is always with me, so she couldn't look in that.

I guess Mom looked in my room sometimes. I guess most mothers do. If you want to have secrets, you can't keep them anywhere in the house because the bottom line is *the house is not yours it is theirs.*

The bottom line is even if you love your mom (or your aunt), *you can't trust them.*

For sure, the McCartys think that they can't trust me now. (They can't.) They think I'm emotionally unstable. (I am!) Probably I have a cache of drugs hidden somewhere in my room. (Wish I did! But I'm too smart to keep drugs in my room.)

All this while my uncle is saying how Dr. Freer telephoned my aunt, told her that she suspected me since the paperweight was missing after my hour with her, but she'd decided to wait until my next appointment, thinking that I might return the paperweight, but I've been canceling my appointments. And so . . .

"Dr. Freer is disappointed, Jenna. But not angry. She has

asked Caroline to come with you to your next appointment with her, when you can return the paperweight and explain . . ."

What? What's Uncle Dwight saying?

". . . in fact Dr. Freer thinks your action might be a major breakthrough, since prior to this, you've been severely re-pressed and uncommunicative. . . ."

The blood in my ears is pounding harder. I'm sitting with my arms folded tight, clutching at my sides. *Go to hell! All of you!* In another room a TV is playing. Mikey's after-school cartoons. I wonder if when I see Aunt Caroline, she will smile sadly at me and wait for me to apologize, and if I do, she will hug me and cry over me.

Let them love you in my place. Please, Jenna.

"I'm not going back to Dr. Freer. Nobody can make me."

"Jenna! How can you—"

"I'm not! *I am not.*"

Suddenly it's like we're trapped together. Or we've fallen into the water together, flailing against each other and strug-gling not to drown. Uncle Dwight is scolding me, and I'm saying okay then, send me away, and he says of course no one is going to send me away, and I say, "But you don't want me, do you? Why would you want me?" and Uncle Dwight says, "Of course we want you, Jenna, we love you," and I'm laughing to hear this—*love! we love you!*—for why would anybody love me if they knew me? I'm on my feet, and Uncle Dwight is on his feet, and our voices are raised, and there's a look on Uncle Dwight's face like he's wary and guarded and frightened of me, for what if I begin to scream, I'm so impulsive and emotional, so unstable, can't be trusted. I'm saying in this really nasty voice that's a copy of Trina's voice when she spoke to her mother, "You aren't really my uncle; it's just Aunt Caroline who is my aunt," and quickly he says, "That's ridiculous, Jenna, of course I'm your uncle, you are my niece, I've known you for most of your life," and this is a surprise to me, that Uncle Dwight would say such a thing, and I realize that it's true: This man has known me most of my life, and I've hardly given him a thought and could not say the color of his eyes or guess his age. And I say, "I don't want you to love me! If you knew me, you wouldn't love me! I steal things, and I do worse things, *you and Aunt Caroline don't know.*"

Uncle Dwight stares at me—I'm so like Trina quivering with some kind of weird rage. I'm clumsy, colliding with a chair that I almost knock over when I turn to run out of the room.

10

Won't. Can't make me.
  Don't love me—I don't love you.
  The blue sky I wanted.
  Send me away then.
  (Where?)

11

It's the day after my uncle and the glass paperweight. It's the day after my aunt tried to speak with me, but I shunned her and ran to my room. It's the day after the night I decided I could not run away because maybe I did love them, maybe they loved me. Somehow Crow would know this. Crow would say, Chérie! *Take care, it's a big step to the street*. I've been watching for Crow from inside school. From my hidden place. Even if Crow glanced in my direction when he left the building alone, headed for his motorcycle parked in its usual place against the rear chain-link fence, even if he turned to stare toward me, sensing that someone is watching him, even then he wouldn't see me because I am not visible.

"I wish."

12

Here's how it ends.

My aunt and my uncle say okay, I can return the paper-weight to Dr. Freer by mail.

I tell them THANK YOU.

(I am sincere, not sarcastic.)

(I mean I am *truly* sincere, not sarcastic.)

In the kitchen, where Aunt Caroline can look on (if she wishes, I'm not trying to hide anything), I wrap the beautiful glass paperweight in tissue paper so it can't crack. There's a gift box Aunt Caroline has given me out of a closet. This also has tissue paper in it. Carefully I place the paperweight in the box. I ask Aunt Caroline if I can have three lemons out of the refrigerator, and Aunt Caroline is surprised but says, "Why, certainly, Jenna. I wasn't planning on using lemons tonight."

"Thank you, Aunt Caroline. I really appreciate it."

By this time Becky and Mikey have joined me. So curious about what Jenna is doing!

The lemons are bright yellow, just the right size to fit in my hand. Somehow, you never look at lemons. (Who looks at lemons?) But these lemons are beautiful, I think. Crow would wonder what I was doing the way my aunt and my little cousins are wondering, but he wouldn't judge me, the way he doesn't judge his father.

From Crow I am learning (I am beginning to learn) it isn't perfect people you love but people you know, you love.

It's a long way to loving my dad, though. For sure.

Upstairs in my room I tried to write an apology to Dr. Freer, but it sounded so phony, I hated it. This is a better way, I think. On one of the lemons I print, with a red marker pen, "SHAME." On another lemon I write, with a black marker pen, "SORRY." On the third lemon I write, with a green marker pen, "DON'T KNOW WHY/ JENNA."

These three lemons I place inside the box. More tissue paper; then I shut the box and wrap it in tinsel-colored paper (left over from Christmas, but you can't tell, the paper hasn't been torn or wrinkled), place it inside a larger, brown mailing box, and address it to "DR. MEGHAN T. FREER" at her office on Summit Street.

My little cousins are utterly mystified. Why lemons, why am I mailing lemons, who is Dr. Freer? Aunt Caroline shakes her head, says, "Why, Jenna! What a strange way of . . ." then changes her mind and says, "What a good idea, Jenna. Thank you."

I mark the box "FIRST CLASS PRIORITY MAIL." It will be expensive, but I'll pay for the postage myself.

13

In April, this happens.

Early April there's still snow. Broken slabs of bluish ice at the lake. Trina Holland is friends with me again—I guess—kind of hurtful, pinching my arm to make it bruise: "Baby, lookin' *good*." Sure I've been anxious. Trina hasn't called me much, so when she does, one night when I'm in my room doing homework, saying there's these really cool older guys who want to hang out with us, at somebody's grandparents' lodge at Yarrow Lake, where they broke in, these are "fantastically cool" guys Trina has met through T-Man, "so, Jenna, come outside, and we'll pick you up in, like ten minutes, is that cool?" quickly I say, "All right," I hear myself say, "All right," and Trina says, "Okay, baby, but know what? You can bring something, like, for the party, like I am," and I don't know what Trina means, Trina clicks off, so I can't ask her. Then I'm laughing I'm so excited, unless I'm panicked, thinking, *I can't do this, can't sneak out* except I'm thinking, *Maybe Crow will be there—Crow is an older guy.* I'm throwing on clothes, washing my face and slapping on makeup like Trina's, makeup that comes in a tube, and lipstick, midnight plum, which is Trina's totally cool/sexy lipstick that completely changes my face, because without makeup my face is washed-out and plain and I hate it, but with makeup I'm okay-looking, I guess.

Lookin' good, Trina says. That sharp look in Trina's eyes meaning she likes me again, just barely.

I'm wearing jeans, boots, a cable-knit sweater over a T-shirt. My down-filled jacket with the hood.

Sneaking out of the house! I've sort of done this before, slipping out without telling anybody where I'm going, but during the day, not at almost eleven o'clock at night. A school night. Trying not to laugh, I'm so nervous. This is weeks after the thing with Dr. Freer, my aunt and my uncle trust me again or anyway act like they do, if they have doubts, they keep them secret from me. Nobody will see that I'm gone, I've shut the door to my room and the lights are out inside, nobody will knock on my door—they'll be thinking I've gone to bed. Anyway, I think only Uncle Dwight is still up, watching TV news downstairs. On my way out the back door, I sneak into the dining room, where there's a cabinet with wine bottles, liquor, mixes, so I reach inside, to the back row of bottles, where I figure whatever I take won't be missed, and my fingers close on a heavy long-necked bottle, Smirnoff vodka.

"Trina, this is a mistake maybe . . ."

"Chill out. Nobody's gonna babysit you."

At first at the party Trina is edgy too, nobody's paying much attention to us, even T-Man who's hanging out with the guys from Lebanon. There's Gil Rathke, who's a big-muscled guy in his twenties with a shaved head and a wiry little beard, there's Ross Skaggs, who is maybe older, a loud barking laugh and a gap in his lower teeth like one is missing, another guy people call Osk (like Oscar?) and of the guys, we know only T-Man and Jax Yardman, who are trying to act important. Of the girls, there's only Dolores who we know, the others are older, like in their twenties, their names are Audra, Nancy, Lindy, Marcia, and they work at a hair salon in town, one of them's a dental assistant, one works at the 7-Eleven out on Route 35, which was where, just a few hours ago, the guys met her, invited her to the lake to the party, except she has a two-year-old at home, wants to tell people about him in a guilty-drunken voice but the party is too loud, music too loud, it's a

German heavy metal rock band that's like spikes through your head, nobody wants to listen to her, including me.

"Baby-Mousie, let's *dance*."

Mousie is a name the new guys are calling me. Like, nobody knows that I am Jenna. Trina has told them I'm seventeen, like her. Still, I look kind of young. The youngest at the party. This guy with a buzz cut and a look to his face like it's been singed in a fire is asking am I "Mousie" all over or just where you can see, and I'm laughing too hard to answer, so Trina answers for me: "That's for us to know and you to find out, see?" Trina is dancing with me, Trina is teasing how clumsy I am, dizzy-dazed though I have not been smoking weed like the others, only just drinking, one slow sip at a time from a plastic cup because I am worried about being so far from home. T-Man drove for miles to Yarrow Lake, not the usual way but back roads, this isn't a part of Yarrow Lake known to me, not many houses close by and everything so dark. By moonlight you can see the lake, which is beginning to thaw in the daytime but at the shore there are sharp-looking slabs and layers of ice. This place we're in, it's freezing cold except where there's space heaters turned on high and the wire coils are fiery red. The guys tried to start a fire in the big stone fireplace, but there's mostly garbage in it, the kindling is wet, logs are wet, there isn't much fire, only smoldering, and the chimney must be blocked so smoke is backing up into the room, so windows have to be opened, doors are opened, there's a sound of glass breaking like somebody got impatient and broke out a window. Trina is handing me another "zombie cola," which she says is basically vodka so okay for her and me both, in case somebody smells our breaths, like Trina's mom, or my aunt and uncle, it won't be detected like other drinks with a stronger smell. "And if, like, that happens, Baby-Mousie, you leave me out of it, okay?" Trina is twisting my wrist like she's teasing, but actually it hurts. One of Gil Rathke's friends with eyes like headlights and giving off heat like the fiery red coils wants to dance with both Trina and me at the same time, but my legs are too clumsy, so it's just him and Trina careening around the room, shouting with laughter.

My head is so dizzy; I'm trying to stop the spinning by lying on a leather sofa pushed back against a wall and shutting my eyes. There's a buzzing in my head like electricity. I'm beginning to worry I will be sick to my stomach, the zombie colas are so strong. If I am sick, Trina will be disgusted with me, and the guys will laugh at me, I will be so ashamed. A while ago one of the older girls, I think her name was Audra, pressed her hand against my forehead, saying I didn't look so great and how old was I, who brought me here, but Trina told her, chill out, Mousie is cool.

Don't see Audra now. She hooked up with one of the Lebanon guys and is gone.

This is wild: Two drunk guys are trying to dislodge the mounted deer head that's on the wall above the fireplace. I've been staring at this deer head, it looks so alive. Beautiful antlers like a spreading tree. Glassy eyes fixed on me. *I was alive once, like you. Your turn is coming.*

One of the drunk guys prods at the deer head with a poker, like he's attacking the deer, yelling and stamping his feet, so suddenly the head comes loose and crashes to the floor, antlers and all. Everybody is laughing like hyenas except Gil Rathke, he's pissed because this is his grandpa's place and he doesn't want it trashed.

Later, Trina and Dolores are freaky dancing. The guys are really into watching. Somebody I never saw before, with what looks like a dagger tattoo on the back of his hand, is hunched over me, calling, "Mous-sie," trying to pull me to my feet, but I'm still feeling kind of sickish.

A shaved-head guy says, "I'm not feeling it. She's too young."

It's then I notice that not just Audra is gone but the other older girls. Some of the guys too. For a long time people were coming in, going out and coming in, but now there aren't more than five or six guys. Then Dolores is gone. Now there's just Trina and me and these guys I don't know. T-Man is gone, Jax Yardman must be gone. There's a look in the lodge of broken things. There's a smell of burned garbage. My eyes are watering from the smoke. Outside, there's the noise of a motor-cycle revving up, and I'm thinking, *Crow is here, Crow will take me home.* Maybe all this time I have been waiting for Crow, thinking that he will take me home. Though I know that Crow won't be here. I know that Crow won't be taking me home. Why is T-Man gone, wasn't T-Man supposed to take us home . . . ? In spite of the cold, Trina is dancing barefoot. She's in just a little tank top, jeans. Sexy/skinny legs. Lately Trina has been letting her hair grow in, it's a mix of ash blond, dishwater blond, brown, and streaks of purple. Trina's face is slick with sweat like oil, and as she dances, she throws her head from side to side as if she wants to break her neck, she's flailing her arms that are painful to see, they're so thin. The German rock band is getting louder, and Trina is dancing harder like electricity is coursing through her, she can't stop.

Then Trina is squealing, guys are lifting her. Carrying her into a back room, and she's squealing and kicking like it's a game. The buzz-cut guy with drunk eyes and a snout look to his face like a pig is trying to lift me, calling me Mous-sie and squeezing my left breast so hard I'm whimpering in pain. The guy named Ross is helping him except suddenly I'm starting to vomit, a hot clot of something acid comes up into my mouth, I'm gagging, spitting and choking, and the guys drop me quick, letting me fall back onto the sofa and onto the floor, disgusted.

The floor is so cold, I'm pressing my hot face against it. I can't stop coughing. There's something sticky in my hair. There's something sticky on the front of my cable-knit sweater that my aunt bought me for Christmas. My jeans are torn in front. One of my boots is missing. I'm trying to crawl somewhere, to hide. The broken deer head is on the floor a few feet away, one of its glass eyes is gone. I can hear Trina screaming. The guys are shouting with laughter and excitement. It's the hyena laughter that scares me. I'm stumbling, trying not to fall. I'm in the doorway, seeing Trina naked on a grungy carpet on the floor, scissor kicking as the guys hunch over her, she's crying, really crying, I'm saying, "Let her alone! Don't hurt her!" and one of the guys rushes at me and shoves me away, shuts the door in my face. I'm so scared, I'm pounding on the door with my fists shouting for them to let Trina alone, but nobody pays attention to me, so I run from the lodge, stumbling in the snow and ice, desperate to get help for Trina. I don't have my cell phone, I'm missing my left boot, so scared the guys will come after me and hurt me, in a panic staggering through underbrush to a lakeside house about a hundred yards away, where earlier this evening lights were burning, I'm pounding on the door, begging for whoever is inside to open the door, after an excruciating few minutes a light is switched on overhead, and an older man opens the door astonished to see me, I'm pleading for him to please help us, please call the police, my friend is being hurt.

14

. . . in the Yarrow Lake Medical Center vehicle jolting and lurching along the unpaved road to the highway, siren shrieking over our heads like a deranged seabird, the medics allow me to hold Trina's hand, she's moaning and writhing on a stretcher, covered in blankets, strapped in place, half conscious, sobbing, her thin cold fingers clutching at mine and her swollen, bleeding mouth moving almost inaudibly: *Don't let me go, Jenna, stay with me.*

15

Think of the places you *aren't*.

Places from which you are *absent*.

Like, if it's a school day and you aren't in school. And your homeroom desk is empty. And your homeroom teacher stares at the empty desk, blinking and distracted because she has heard that something has happened to you, that's why no one is seated in your desk this morning.

Each desk, in each class, through the school day. An empty desk. By midmorning word is starting to spread about what happened to you and Trina Holland the previous night, by the end of the day everyone knows, or knows something.

Trina Holland, brought by ambulance to Yarrow Lake Medical Center sometime after midnight.

Jennifer Abbott, in "police custody."

Whatever happened happened at the lake.

A party, drugs and drinking, older guys, drug dealers from

Lebanon, maybe Trina and you both OD'd on Ecstasy, or crystal meth, or heroin. Maybe you were both gang-raped and beaten. Maybe police arrested all of you in a drug raid.

T-Man Dubie and Jax Yardman are absent from their classes too. Maybe, last night, partying with her drug dealer friends, Trina Holland went too far, finally. Maybe the spoiled rich girl is being punished like she deserves. And you with her.

". . . 'stable condition,' we've been told. We won't be able to question Trina for another day at least. So, Jennifer—"

Stable condition! I'm so grateful to hear this, the rest of the detective's words hardly register.

"—what happened last night that you witnessed? That you can describe to us, in detail. Please take your time, Jennifer. This is very . . ."

Two Yarrow Lake detectives, middle-aged. Looking more like schoolteachers than cops. The woman is the one who mostly addresses me, calling me *Jennifer*. As often as she can: *Jennifer*.

Because I'm looking so young, I guess. Shivery and scared. A stark-white square Band-Aid on my forehead above my bruised right eye. My mouth swollen. Something clotted and nasty in my hair that needs to be shampooed and combed out, soon.

Jennifer is a technique, you could call it a trick, to make a witness feel less anxious. A "material witness" to a crime. In this case, to crimes. The detectives must make the witness feel that they are to be trusted.

To make me feel, if I give the names of the guys who assaulted Trina Holland, I won't be in danger.

Because I'm fifteen, a minor, my aunt Caroline McCarty has accompanied me to police headquarters. Poor Aunt Caroline! Looking stunned still. Her shock at seeing me last night, 2:40 A.M., in the bright fluorescent-lit emergency room—my face puffy and swollen and wet with tears and the bandage on my forehead where somehow I'd been cut, and my swollen mouth, where somehow I'd been punched by a guy's fist, and my hair, and the heather-colored cable-knit sweater she'd given me for Christmas, clotted with vomit— this shock is still in Aunt Caroline's eyes as she stares at me.

Until the call came from Yarrow Lake police, waking them from their sleep, the McCartys had thought their niece Jenna was asleep in her room as usual. Where else could she be?

Not *Jenna, how could you?* We're beyond that now.

Not *Jenna, how could you? How, when we love you?*

". . . as you know, arrests were made at the scene, but there may be others involved who escaped before the officers arrived. We understand that you're upset and confused and probably don't know the identities of most of the men, but we need to know as much as you can provide, Jennifer. Until Trina Holland is able to give a statement, you are our sole witness. For the time being, rest assured that your testimony will be held in strictest confidence."

I'm shivering, I am so cold. So scared. Absent from school on a school day means something special, but this "something special" isn't a good thing.

For the time being. Strictest confidence.

When I shut my eyes, it's Trina I see: her small naked body on the filthy floor like something flung down, a naked doll. Trina is screaming for the guys to let her alone, and the guys are laughing at her, and one of them rushes at me with a look of fury like he wants to kill me, shoving me back, slamming the door in my face. . . .

Sure, I'm scared. What they might do to me if I inform on them.

Gil Rathke. Ross Skaggs. "Osk." The guy with the buzz cut and the singed-looking skin, calling me Mousie and squeezing my left breast like he wanted to twist it off my body.

In the ER the hurt breast was examined. Already turning purplish orange, ugly. Aunt Caroline was told but has not seen. Aunt Caroline has been told a number of things but has not seen.

". . . unlikely event of a trial. Five of the suspects are in custody and being interrogated, in cases like this the usual procedure is . . ."

Unlikely event of a trial! I don't understand this but hope that this will be so.

My mouth feels numb, my upper lip is swollen. When I try to speak, my voice sounds like something rusted. I will tell the detectives what I remember: It happened so fast.

How they turned on us. On Trina.

How in, like, a few seconds everything changed. Like a match lighted and held to flammable material.

Must've been speed, crystal meth. Must've been more than just drinking and smoking weed. "Wasted," "smashed," "smashed out of their skulls"—that's what I saw.

Happened so fast!

Once started, couldn't be stopped!

I guess, yes. I'd been drinking too.

Not drugs, only just . . .

"Zombie colas." Vodka plus Diet Coke.

Something else in the drinks? Maybe . . .

. . . from my uncle's liquor cabinet. The vodka.

No, not usually. Not hard liquor. Mostly beer . . .

Not ever before. Not anything I'd taken from . . .

Not liquor, or money. Some pills: OxyContin. From my uncle's medicine drawer.

Last year. Last fall. No.

He never discovered the pills missing, it was an old prescription.

Just myself. Except for one I gave to Trina Holland.

Just that once. To Trina. Because . . .

Yes. I guess. Pretty often . . .

Christmas Eve, that was . . .

. . . an accident, I didn't mean . . .

. . . a boy at the high school, a senior . . .

. . . friend of Trina's, Jax Yardman . . .

. . . T-Man Dubie, don't know his first name . . .

No. Not like last night. Not ever.

Older guys: Gil Rathke, Ross Skaggs, "Osk." From Lebanon. The others I don't . . .

. . . could recognize them, yes. I guess.

Through Trina, it was Trina's . . .

. . . Trina's friends . . .

. . . heard her scream, pushed open the door, saw . . .

* * *

My statement to the Yarrow Lake police detectives takes all morning. My statement is recorded on tape. My statement is all the truth I know about what happened to Trina Holland in the lodge at Yarrow Lake sometime after midnight of April 7, 2005. By the time my statement is completed, my voice is almost gone. My head is pulsing with pain. My aunt Caroline has had to excuse herself to leave the interview room, she's so upset.

But when the detectives escort me from the room a while later, Aunt Caroline is waiting for me in an outer room. Managing to smile though her eyes are still stunned. She takes my hands in hers, she hugs me. So tight, it's like she's fearful I might be torn from her. Saying only "Let's go home, Jenna. You must be exhausted."

16

So sorry didn't mean
   don't know why
  feel so bad . . .
     not ever again
      not ever again
       not ever again
        NOT EVER AGAIN

17

"Hello? Hello? He*llo*? Is that—Trina?"

The line clicks dead. It's Trina's cell phone—at least it's Trina's number I've called—but no one answers when my call goes through.

Next time I call, the screen reads UNAVAILABLE.

One of the guys might've taken Trina's cell. One of the guys who hasn't been arrested yet. I guess the police would know this?

Can't call Trina Holland in the Yarrow Lake Medical Center; her phone is blocked to incoming calls. Can't visit Trina, no visitors are wanted. I send a card, "THINKING OF YOU GET WELL SOON," and a dozen purple-plum crepe paper flowers I make myself, needing something to do to distract myself the five days I am home from school, something with my hands that I can see, something that's meant to make people smile, but I guess it's not the right thing for Trina, Trina never replies.

My aunt calls Trina's mother, but no one ever answers. There is no voice mail either.

I am wondering how badly Trina was hurt. If you call the medical center, the operator says she can't "reveal" this information. If you call the Yarrow Lake police, it's the same.

On the front page of the *Yarrow Lake Journal* is a single-column article with the headline

5 AREA YOUTHS ARRESTED FOLLOWING ASSAULT
YARROW LAKE GIRL, 17, HOSPITALIZED

Trina's name isn't given, of course. There are three grainy photographs of "alleged assailants" Gil Rathke, Ross Skaggs, Oscar Tybek, aged twenty-six, twenty-seven, twenty-four respectively.

Even Detective Pelka, who'd seemed to like me, when I call her at the number she gave me only repeats in a neutral voice what has been released to the media: The "suspects" are in custody, the case is being "investigated."

"But—I'm Jennifer Abbott! Trina's friend, who was with her at—"

Detective Pelka says curtly, "Jennifer, I know who you are.

But I can't tell you anything more. Our information regarding Trina Holland is confidential."

"Even Trina's health? Like—is she *okay*?"

Detective Pelka doesn't answer at first. Maybe she's exasperated with me. I'm thinking, *Trina is on life support, Trina is dying,* but then the detective says in a voice sounding now like controlled anger, "You'll be hearing about your friend soon enough, Jennifer."

18

april 15

hey baby

we relly screwd up didnt we!
thanks for saving my stupid life
(i gues)

you were the best friend i ever had (i gues)
i was a shitty friend but its too late now
i'm sorry (?)
maybe i'm not sorry, i'm taking Percs
my nose is broken & has to be "repared"
i look like shit & a Perc makes me laugh
i wont be coming back to YHS (big deal)

my bitch mother is moving us to tuxedo park ny
my Grandparents live in tuxedo park its VERY BORING

see, I'm leaveing without saying goodbye
not one person here not even crow

not even you, if you saved my life
can't see anybody without them seeing me &
thinking what happened to her!!!
& they would think that bitch deseved it
& they would be right

baby you screwed up bad as me
shouldve run away & hid
the guys wouldve taken care of me afterward
wouldnt let me alone there to freeze
(i gues)

i dont want to see you again ever
maybe i hate you, screwing us both up
calling cops is RATTING

i gues you wanted to help me
i'm not any RAT
i'm sorry thats how it is possable for me
it isnt possable for me another way

your card & flowers i ripped into pieces
Percs make you laugh & laugh & you get tired & sleep
i wont miss anybody there not even crow

its cool, I am getting a new face not in this
shitty hospital but in new york where theres
worldclass surgons   cosmic surgons can repare
a broke face beter than new

my cheekbone was broke also my (right) eye socket
it wasnt gil who kicked me, some guy with steel toe boots

Hey baby if you saw me anyway with my new face
        when its fixed you wouldn't know me
if you hadnt puked baby youd have a cool new face
        coming too!!!

love & kisses & dont forget me too soon

trina

p.s. tell crow tuxedo park has got this stone
wall around it like alcatraz, to keep out bikers

19

Here is a surprise.

The five days I have to stay home from school, my teachers e-mail me, even Mr. Farrell, who I thought totally hated me, and Mr. Feldman, who says he will help me with our algebra assignments when I return. My homeroom teacher, Mrs. Terricotte, calls to ask how I am, saying she misses me, everybody in homeroom misses me, which I can't believe is true, but it's nice of her to say, and our gym teacher, Dara Bowen, calls to talk the longest, saying how courageous I was to run for help for my friend, how courageous to testify against the men who raped and assaulted Trina Holland, and a panicky sensation washes over me: *How does she know? Does everybody know?* for the police had assured the McCartys and me that my statement would be confidential unless there is a trial, and a trial isn't expected. . . . And when a week later it turns out that Trina is refusing to press charges, refusing to identify Gil Rathke and his friends, refusing even to speak with detectives, Ms. Bowen asks to speak with me in her office after gym class, upset like I have never seen her. "This will only send a signal guys can get away with rape. Jenna, you must try to talk sense into her. The two of you can testify together, the community will support you! If it's Trina's parents who are persuading her not to talk . . ." and I say, "Ms. Bowen, Trina is gone from Yarrow Lake. She won't ever be back."

It's like Trina said in her e-mail. Her mother took her away to live with her grandparents. There is no law to force a victim of any crime to make a statement to police or even to speak with police.

Tuxedo Park, New York! That's near Tarrytown. Like Trina Holland and Jenna Abbott have traded places.

I printed out Trina's e-mail to me, to keep. But I won't show it to anyone, not even my aunt. It's Trina's first e-mail to me, and I understand that it will be the last, Trina just isn't into sitting still long enough to write text messages you need to coordinate your fingers and your brain to type.

20

"Jenna! Good news."

It's my uncle who tells me this: There won't be any trial, no need for me to testify against Gil Rathke and his friends.

I won't need to be publicly "courageous" after all.

The sexual assault charges against the men have been dropped because Trina, the primary victim, refused to give a statement to police. So county prosecutors decided to discount my statement too. Gil Rathke and his friends have pleaded guilty to reduced charges: trespassing, breaking and entering, aiding and abetting underage drinking, resisting arrest, possession of controlled substances (marijuana, crystal meth), and possession of an unlicensed handgun (a .38-caliber revolver was discovered by police under the driver's seat of Rathke's TrailBlazer).

A .38-caliber revolver! I'm stunned. At the lake, in the lodge that night, those hours I was there . . .

"You didn't know, Jenna? Did you?

Not with his eyes, for he doesn't trust me, but with his mouth Uncle Dwight is smiling. Like he's giving me an opportunity to say something to redeem myself.

"No, Uncle Dwight. I didn't know."

"Do you think your friend Trina knew?"

The gun, Uncle Dwight means. Did Trina know? Suddenly I'm filled with rage at Trina.

If she knew, or didn't know. If she knew, and didn't care.

These really cool older guys . . .

The mistake is hanging out with Trina Holland.

What can I tell my uncle that he'd believe? Ever again? From me? After I've stolen from him, lied to him? Insulted him?

I say, wiping at my eyes, "She wasn't my friend, Uncle Dwight. It was my fault for trusting her."

It's the right answer, I guess. My uncle seems to think so.

21

Another surprise: Dad comes to see me.

Three days Dad plans to spend in New Hampshire. Though it's a very busy season for him, a "frantic" time, in fact, he has cleared away three days on his April calendar to spend in New Hampshire. (The McCartys invited Dad to stay with them, but he prefers the historic four-star Buttrick Inn twenty miles away in Hanover.) Dad is looking older, thicker jawed, his eyes are wary and guarded, assessing me, but he's tan, and his hair is darker than I remember, attractively threaded with gray. The first time Dad sees me, he hugs me tight, like you'd expect from a father who hasn't seen his daughter for months, but there's something forced and stiff about his arms around me, like he isn't certain who I am.

Still, being hugged by Dad. Tears spill out of my eyes.

Like I am "emotional" when *I am not*.

Dad has rented a BMW at the Hanover airport, he takes us

on a slow drive along Yarrow Lake, into the foothills of the White Mountains. Dinner at the Buttrick Inn. Next day, lunch at the Boathouse on Yarrow Lake. Much of our conversation is Dad talking about La Jolla, the new house, new family, recent very successful business trips abroad. Instead of murmuring, *That's great, Dad*, or *Wow, Dad!* I'm just kind of quiet.

Funny how, the more a person talks, the less he can say.

So much is unspoken between us—for instance, Mom, the wreck, the incident at Yarrow Lake. It's like we are two blind people groping for each other but missing. Dad is trying not to openly express his frustration and disgust with his daughter, screwing up again.

Maybe he'd like to grab me and shake me, hard. The way he grabbed and shook me at the Tarrytown rehab clinic.

The last time we touched. I remember.

We're cruising along a state highway a few miles east of Yarrow Lake. Actually it doesn't matter where we are, we're confined together. Father, daughter. What did Crow say?: Your father is always your father, that doesn't change. Dad brings up the subject of my moving to La Jolla, not exactly a new, unique subject, and I shift a little lower in my seat, saying nothing. Next, Dad brings up the subject of my seeing a really good psychiatrist—not a psychologist—and I don't say anything.

I'm waiting for Dad to ask about Dr. Freer. But maybe he's forgotten her name. Maybe the McCartys never informed him that I'd stopped seeing Dr. Freer. And the reason why I'd stopped.

"Also, Jenna. Rehab."

"Rehab? What kind of rehab?"

"Honey, you know what kind. Obviously."

Driving, Dad gropes for my hand to squeeze, can't quite find it so has to content himself with just touching my wrist, with some force.

I'm scared. I don't know what Dad means. Drugs?

"But—I'm not using drugs, Dad."

Dad laughs loudly. "Hey, c'mon, Jenna, this is me, your dad. The McCartys might not think you have a serious drug problem, but you and I know better, eh?"

Dad is smiling a kind of lewd, ghastly smile like he's such a cool dude he knows the secret life of the fifteen-year-old screwup druggie. A feeling like flame comes over my brain.

"Dad, I said I'm not using drugs. I'm *not*."

"Which is why, on Christmas Eve, you had to be taken to the emergency room to have your stomach pumped? Which is why fifteen days ago you were partying with adult drug dealers? Until they turned on you and . . ."

Dad's foot is pressing down on the gas pedal of the BMW. We're moving now at about sixty-five miles an hour. To our right is the western edge of Mascoma Lake. I'm anxious there might be a bridge somewhere ahead. Dad has been working himself up to this, two martinis at lunch. That lewd, ghastly grin crinkling his tanned face. What he wants to ask is *Did you have sex with the drug dealers? Are you still a virgin?*

My fingers close over the handle of the passenger-side door. My heart is beating so hard, I can't think clearly.

Just then Dad's cell phone rings. It's a call from his New York office. Something has just come up, some crisis having to do with negotiations in Beijing.

In the end Dad leaves that afternoon for New York. Two days in New Hampshire are enough.

Then, this happens.

It's an afternoon near the end of April, a warm, drizzly day, my mistake is I'm leaving school alone, and once I'm off school property, from out of nowhere the guys surround me, like they've been waiting for me: T-Man, Rust, Jax Yardman. T-Man and Jax are tall and looming. One of them bumps into me from behind, another leans into my face, sneering, "Rat-girl, you got our friends in trouble. Now you're in trouble." And Jax Yardman making a sucking noise with his lips, glaring at me belligerently.

I push past them, walking quickly. I don't say a word to them, I'm looking straight ahead. I know better than to run, for that would only provoke them to chase me, like dogs. I tell myself, *They won't hurt me. They won't touch me.*

Of the names they call me, "rat" is the nicest.

"Hey, assholes, back off."

It's Crow, on his Harley-Davidson.

It's Crow, braking the skidding motorcycle to a stop, jumping off in a fury to yell at his friends, ex-friends, they must be. By this time I'm pretty scared. Trembling and trying not to cry. Guys yelling at one another, pushing at one another.

What happens is confused, clumsy.

In this residential neighborhood across from the grounds of Yarrow High, it looks weird, like something on TV that has spilled out into real life.

At first Crow and T-Man are shoving at each other. Then they're throwing punches. Like a crafty little dog, Rust is circling behind Crow to attack him, except Crow turns suddenly to shove him, hard. Jax is trying to hit Crow from behind T-Man—suddenly he's on the ground, looking stunned. Rust is backing off, squinting and cringing as if he's been hurt. Crow has hit T-Man in the face and bloodied his nose. T-Man kicks furiously at Crow's legs, Crow lunges into him so hard, T-Man loses his balance and falls heavily to the ground. T-Man and Jax scramble to their feet. Rust is panting through his mouth, backing away. Crow is excited and agitated, advancing on them with his fists raised, but they don't want to fight anymore.

Crow climbs back onto his motorcycle, which has been idling at the curb, and drives in triumph to where I'm standing. He's breathing hard, his face is flushed and sweaty. There's a thread of bright blood leaking from his left nostril, and the front of his black leather jacket is speckled with blood. He's smiling at me. "Climb on, *chérie*. I'll take you out of here."

I tell Crow I can't. Can't ride on a motorcycle.

"Why not?"

I just can't. I'm afraid.

Crow laughs, sounding like his father. "Hell, I'm afraid too. I don't let that stop me. C'mon."

After the wreck, the terrible wreck, I can't. Can't.

Except somehow, shutting my eyes like jumping off a high board into water below, I do.

22

"Hang on tight, *chérie*."

Oh! oh! oh! — my breath is snatched from me, the wind is rushing against my face.

Tightening my arms around Crow's waist. Holding Crow, holding on to Crow as I have never held on to anyone in my life.

Crow in his blood-splattered leather jacket, jeans, and biker boots. Crow with the coiled-snake tattoo at his wrist, smiling into the wind like it's his friend, nothing to fear.

This wild ride. This ride through the familiar streets of Yarrow Lake suddenly unfamiliar as if seen through the wrong end of a telescope, whipping past. *Oh! oh!* as Crow turns, banks the motorcycle into the wind, and we're headed away from Yarrow High and residential streets. We're on a blacktop road bordered on one side by open, undeveloped land, newly budded willow trees rushing past in a dreamy shimmer of green. Before I have time to prepare, to react, we're up onto, then over, a rattly wood-plank bridge over a small stream where sunlight glitters like broken glass below.

"You okay, *chérie*? Want to turn back?"

In the rearview mirror that's stippled with rust, I can see Crow's face, Crow's smiling eyes searching for me. Quickly I tell Crow that I'm not afraid, I don't want to turn back.

Later I will wonder if Crow doesn't always remember my name.

For a guy who knows so many girls and women, it's easier to call them *chérie*.

I'm not thinking such thoughts now, hunched behind Crow, trying to catch my breath, staring with damp astonished eyes.

How low to the ground we are! How open to the wind, to the pavement rushing beneath! How wide the driver's seat is directly in front of me, the sheepskin saddle I must grip with my knees, awkwardly. As if my legs are being pried open. The raw keening roar of the motor that makes my heart race. Sets my teeth on edge. It's like Crow is a black flame rushing through the landscape, and I am being carried with him like a trusting child, my hair whipping in the wind and my eyes streaming tears. I don't have time to think of the other girls who've ridden behind Gabriel Saint-Croix on this motorcycle, if they gripped him tight as I am gripping him, astonished by my own boldness. Don't have time to wonder *Did they love him too? Were they happy like me?*

This wild ride. I want never to end.

What is hard to become used to is the sky overhead. My eyes keep glancing up, like something's wrong: I'm on a vehicle without a roof. A vehicle without sides to protect the driver and me. No time to think, *Am I afraid? am I terrified?* It's happening too fast for words.

Late April there's a net of glimmering green cast over everything. There's a rich, ripe smell to the air. On the open highway pavement rushed beneath us like a river.

This wild ride, I want never to end.

23

"Try to see, *chérie*. Don't try to remember."

Shutting my eyes. So many times I have tried to remember, but this is the first time I will try just to *see*.

"Keep walking. Don't stop. I can lead you."

Beneath my feet this wood-chip trail is spongy. Last time I was here, back in November, the trail was covered in a crust of snow in places, other stretches were muddy. This afternoon there is a dreamy look to the air, sunlight shifts and ebbs behind banks of filmy clouds. Now that we're off the roaring Harly-Davidson, we can hear birds singing.

Red-winged blackbirds, flocks of them in the cattail marshes beside Sable Creek.

I told Crow that I don't have happy memories of this place, the trail out of Yarrow Lake that runs beside Sable Creek, the footbridge beside the railroad bridge where I panicked and couldn't cross.

Immediately Crow said, "That's where we're going then."

"I don't think—"

"Yes, *chérie*. We will cross the bridge today."

"But . . ."

I've told him about the Tappan Zee Bridge. What happened there, what I saw, or thought I saw, in the lane in front of my mother's car.

Crow shudders. As if bridges trouble him, too.

Softly I say, ". . . can't stop thinking I was meant to die there. With my mom."

These words come out so naturally. Though I have never heard them before.

I expect Crow to challenge what I've said, the way an adult would. But Crow only shivers, as if a shadow has passed over him.

"Lots of places I've felt that way."

There's sadness in Crow's voice, but something blunt and flat too. Meaning *Don't ask me. Not yet.*

Crow has been leading me along the trail, my hand in his. Supposedly, my eyes are shut. In this way I am trying to "see" what was on the Tappan Zee Bridge before the wreck. But I'm cheating. I can see a little, a blurry crescent through my eyelashes.

The swift-running creek. Sunlight on the creek. On the other side, marshes. We've been walking for about ten minutes, Crow has left his motorcycle in a parking lot beside the trail.

Somewhere along here Crow and I first met. When I was new to Yarrow Lake. When I was limping and wincing with pain because I'd tried to run when I wasn't ready yet. *Know what you look like? Somebody who's been in a car crash.*

I don't want to remember how I distrusted Crow then. How I was ready to scream, to run panicked, if he came too close.

Now, Crow is holding my hand.

His fingers are strong and warm, holding my hand.

The bad memory is returning. I've forgotten how wide Sable Creek becomes at this point, joined by another creek flowing in the direction of Yarrow Lake. How ugly the old bridge is, defaced by graffiti.

Crow sees that my eyes are open and chides me, "Hey, girl, you're supposed to be trying to *see*."

Making a game of it. Crow makes games of what he can, failing isn't so serious then.

Bad memories returning. Signs posted along the trail.

NO MOTORCYCLES.

BICYCLES MUST BE WALKED.

NO HORSES.

CAUTION: TRAIN.

"I'm afraid. . . ."

"So?"

"I'm changing my mind, really I don't want—"

"*Chérie*, keep walking. Shut your eyes. We are headed for the bridge. We are going to cross it."

"Gabriel, I don't think—"

"'Gabriel'? Who's he? You think you know 'Gabriel'?"

Crow laughs. I'm not sure what the joke is.

I remember sexy/glamorous Claudette calling him Gabriel. Teasing in a way that seemed cruel. And the look on Crow's face, stricken and somber. A look I've never seen on Crow at any other time.

I don't dare ask Crow about Claudette. I'm summoning up my nerve to ask him about Trina.

"Keep walking, *chérie*. Now, a little hill. I'm your guide. Seeing Eye dog, that's Gabriel."

I'm beginning to be nervous. Through my half-shut eyes I can see the path up the hill, the pedestrian bridge about six feet above. Suddenly this doesn't seem like a good idea, I wish that I'd never agreed to try it.

"Jenna! Come on."

So Crow does know my name. When I'm not *chérie*.

"We're going to cross this bridge when we get to it. Not before and not after."

This makes me laugh, as Crow meant it to. Teasing and playful is Crow's way of coping.

But I'm afraid. I can't keep my eyes shut, the footbridge is so close. . . .

"Last time you were here, and you couldn't cross the bridge, what did you think would happen?"

"I don't know. . . . A train might come along?"

"A train might come along, okay. And then?"

"A train might come along when I was on the bridge. Before I could get across."

"And then?"

"I—I'm not sure."

"Trains come along here all the time, don't they? Obviously, on the track."

This is true. I guess I haven't thought about it.

"What is special about you, Jenna, that the footbridge would collapse because you were on it?"

"I . . . don't know. I'm just scared of bridges."

"The other bridge, the big bridge, you're remembering. Not this little bridge."

Crow is gripping my hand tight. There's an edge in his voice I heard when he spoke to his father. Suddenly we're on the platform above the creek. It's as narrow as I remember it. The wood is as old and rotted-looking as I remember. To our left is the elevated railroad track, about five feet above us. There's the smell of wet wood, the frightening swoosh of water beneath our feet. In March and April, in the spring thaw and after torrential rains, Sable Creek is higher than I've ever seen it.

Not a creek but a river. A furious river deep enough to drown in.

Yet Crow is urging me forward. And I can't.

"*Chérie*, there is no train. I promise you. I can see in both directions: *There is no train.*"

I don't believe him. He isn't even looking. He's laughing at me, I'm such a child to him.

I am a child, I will never grow up. I will never get beyond the bridge. I will never see what is on the bridge, and so I will never cross it.

Crow says, "Let it pass through you, Jenna."

"Let what pass through?"

"Fear."

"It doesn't pass through—it sticks. . . ."

"Make yourself empty, like light. Let fear pass through. Don't let it stick."

"I can't. . . ."

"*I* make myself empty. It's what I do, to cross over."

"You? Why?"

"Every time I risk anything, on the motorcycle, in a place like this, with another person, I'm scared. Because I know things can go wrong, and I can be hurt."

I'm gripping Crow's fingers tight. I can hear his voice quaver, as if the words are being pulled from him.

"I know other people can be hurt. And I hate it."

"'Hate'—what?"

"What the world does to us. Some of us."

Crow sounds angry, disgusted. For a moment I'm frightened of him, the rage quivering in him.

At first Crow isn't going to continue. Then he says, in a low, tense voice, "My brother, Paul, died in an ugly accident when he was thirteen. I was a little kid, just ten. We were living in Maine then. It was before my mother left us—this is why my mother left us. . . . I adored my brother and followed him everywhere he'd let me. Paul and his friends. One day they were jumping and diving into an old stone quarry about a mile from our house, a quarry kids weren't supposed to play in. The water was always cold, even in summer. And deep, except where there were submerged rocks. Paul thought he knew where it was safe to dive and where it wasn't. So he dived from a cliff about twenty feet above the water, hit his head on the edge of a sharp rock, and . . . It was so fast, what happened. One minute Paul was calling to us from the cliff, the next he was in the water, under the water, not moving; it was like his body was broken, just rags. The other boys tried to swim to him, to help him. But they were just kids and panicked. They told me to run for help, and I ran, and ran, I was crying as I ran. . . . I couldn't run fast enough."

Crow swipes at his eyes, his voice trails off.

I tell Crow I'm so sorry. It must have been a nightmare. . . .

"It was. Is."

I've never heard any man speak like Crow has spoken, with such raw anguish. Never seen any man swiping tears from his eyes, his face like something about to break into pieces.

For a long moment we stand in silence. There is nothing that I can say that isn't weak and banal. I am squeezing Crow's fingers, as if to give him strength.

Now Crow nudges me to come with him out onto the foot-bridge. I can't bear to see the creek rushing so close beneath the rotted-looking planks, only a few inches below. "Stop looking! I told you." Crow grips my head in his hands, with his thumbs gently shuts my eyes.

"Stop thinking where you are now. Forget me. Just focus your eyes back onto the Tappan Zee Bridge. We won't move from here. We will be very still. Until you *see*."

Though my eyes are shut, it feels like my eyelids are blinking, quivering. I can't see anything. The noise of the creek rushing beneath my feet is like a roaring in my ears. I am becoming paralyzed with fear, can't stop swallowing. The inside of my mouth feels coated with dust. Mom shifts lanes, we're moving onto the Tappan Zee Bridge. It's a familiar bridge, but very wide. And the Hudson River below, so wide. I'm distracted by something on the dashboard, trying to play a CD, but the disk keeps being rejected, Mom and I have been talking about something, can't remember what, I'm in a sort of peevish mood, don't know why, seems so often I was in this sort of mood not knowing why, and Mom trying to find out, wanting to know, wanting to make me feel better, I guess, but it felt like prying, *Try me, Jenna, maybe I can help*, but I don't want Mom's help, I am fifteen years old, for God's sake, not a little kid, really pissed now the CD won't play, and there is absolutely nothing wrong that I've done, pressing "eject" to try again, suddenly there's something beyond the windshield, something directly in the lane in front of us, I can see it clearly: a bird with wide brown flapping wings? a hawk? a hawk with a darkish head, streaked breast and tail feathers looking dazed as if it has just struck the bridge railing? and I'm screaming for Mom not to hit the hawk, I'm groping for the steering wheel, not knowing what I'm doing, Mom pushes at me, Mom is braking the car, braking too hard, the car swerves, begins to skid toward the railing . . .

Suddenly I *see*. More vividly than I'd seen at the time. More vividly than any dream. My eyes are shut tight, and Crow continues to grip my hands, I'm sobbing with relief: There was something on the bridge after all, I hadn't imagined it, Mom must have seen it too, in that last panicked moment Mom would have understood.

"It was a hawk, Gabriel! A hawk on the bridge."

"A hawk?"

"It must have flown against the railing and was stunned, but managed to recover and fly away. I wanted to protect the hawk, I . . . pulled at the steering wheel—it was there—it really was there! My mother must have seen it too."

Crow holds me, lets me cry. Holds me tight and comforts me as you'd comfort a stricken child. The first time any boy has held me like this. Any man. I am crying as if my heart is broken, which I guess it is.

"I should tell people, shouldn't I? That I saw the hawk, and I pulled at the steering wheel, and it wasn't Mom's fault in any way. . . ."

"Hell, no."

"No—I shouldn't?"

Crow's response is so quick and sure, I'm surprised.

Crow leads me across the footbridge, holding my hand. I feel like a convalescent, learning again to walk. The bridge is still scary, water rushing so close beneath the crude-fitted planks, if I stopped to stare at it, I would become hypnotized, the fear would mount inside me, but Crow pulls me forward—"No train, see?"—no train and the bridge doesn't collapse, and suddenly we're safe on the other side.

I've crossed the footbridge! I feel giddy, exhilarated.

In a rush it comes to me: *I can do anything now.*

This side of Sable Creek the wood-chip trail continues to Yarrow Lake a mile or two away, not visible through the marshy woods. There is nothing unusual about this side, the trail is virtually identical to the trail on the other side. Red-winged blackbirds calling to one another in the cattails, a V formation of Canada geese overhead. These are gunmetal-gray geese, not snow geese. Yet they fly in the same kind of formation, beautiful to observe.

Flying north. Into the blue. Where?

Crow says, "You know it's spring, the geese are migrating north. S'posed to like a colder climate."

My eyes are filling with tears. There's an incandescent look to the sun behind ribbons of cloud gauzy as curtains.

"Hey, Jenna, don't tell anyone about today. It's our secret, see?"

"About the hawk? But—if it's true—"

"Actually, you don't know what's 'true.' If there was a hawk, your mother saw it, so that's cool. Let it go."

"But my father, he has accused Mom of—"

"No. You were hurt in the crash, concussed. Your memory isn't reliable. Like in a dream, your brain gets scrambled. See, I've had concussions too, more than once. In the hospital, on painkillers, your head gets messed up. People confess to things they never did, only dreamed. Terrible things that ruin their lives. Sure, you could try to change your father's mind, but probably he will remember what suits him. That's how people are. You know, and I know. That's our secret. Like my papa. He saw terrible things in Vietnam, maybe he did terrible things, but he doesn't lay that shit on people. He never will."

I'm stunned by this. I know that Crow must be right. But

it's so different from what somebody like Dr. Freer would say: She'd want to discuss the hurt hawk on the bridge, what my feelings were about it, whether I should tell people, etc., for months.

"But—can people forget? It isn't good, is it, to forget?"

"Not talking about something doesn't mean forgetting, Jenna. I will never forget my brother. Nobody in our family will forget Paul. But we don't talk about him. Why'd we want to? He's in our hearts. Like your mom is in your heart."

Crow checks his watch, he has to be getting back to town. He's got work to do in the shop, deliveries to make. I see the green coiled snake just above his wrist, the dark wiry hairs of his forearm. I want to reach out, to touch the tattoo. There is something about it that repels me but fascinates me too.

Crow recrosses the footbridge, taking long strides, like it's no big deal, nothing to be afraid of; like he's forgotten about me, my qualms. He doesn't even glance back at me to see if I'm able to cross the bridge alone.

Of course I can.

"Gabriel, you saved my life."

"Who's 'Gabriel'? *You* saved your life."

I've run to catch up with Crow. Something giddy has come

over me. I'm wiping my eyes, but I'm laughing.

In the parking lot, Crow's motorcycle is the only vehicle. From a distance it looks sleekly powerful; close up it isn't new or shiny but speckled with rust. The sheepskin saddle is frayed and dirty; the black paint on the chassis is chipped. A sensation of faintness comes over me; I will be riding with Crow, behind Crow and with my arms around his waist.

I think *Crow has hypnotized me.*

I think *Crow has given me back my life.*

How to make Crow know that I love him? I will never love anyone the way I love Crow.

Seeing the expression in my face, Crow regards me with a look like he'd give little Roland clamoring to be picked up and held and fussed over. He's smiling like he's happy for me, happy that I am feeling better about myself, but he isn't so happy beneath, maybe. (Now I see the bruised-blue melancholy in Crow's eyes and in the shadowy indentations beneath his eyes like the deeper indentations beneath his father's eyes.) Almost, Crow is annoyed with me. But trying not to show it.

"You wouldn't like me so much, Jenna, if you knew me."

But I do know you! I want to protest.

"I don't believe that. . . ."

"Ask your friend Trina."

This is mean. This is cruel teasing.

"Trina isn't my friend. No longer."

"I thought she was. You didn't listen to me."

"I—I did listen to you. But you used to like Trina too. The two of you got tattoos together—"

"She told you that?"

"The snake. The green snake. There on your arm."

"This I've had for years. Trina went to the mall to get one last year." Crow laughs as if I'm very naive. He's putting the crash helmet on his head. I'm hurt at how he's keeping his distance from me.

"Jenna, I'm leaving Yarrow Lake after graduation."

"Leaving? But—"

It's as if Crow has reached out and slapped me.

"I'm moving to Quebec. I've got lots of relatives there, and I'm going to work with my uncle, who's a cabinetmaker. Also"—Crow pauses, watching me—"Roland is there."

The way Crow says this, an edge to his voice, I know something is wrong.

"See, *chérie*, Roland is my son."

"What? Who—"

"Roland is my son. I'm his father."

"His *father?*"

I sound like someone in a cartoon. I am so totally stunned.

"Claudette, whom you met at my father's shop, she's Roland's mother, she's divorced. I got to know Claudette a few years ago when I was visiting Quebec in the summer. We went out, we hooked up. Claudette's five years older than I am, I think she was just kind of playing with me at first. Then we got serious. . . . Anyway," Crow says abruptly, "Roland is our son."

"Your son! You and . . ."

I'd thought Claudette was Crow's sister!

For a brief while I'd even thought Roland was Mr. Saint-Croix's son.

"We don't always get along, Claudette sees other men. She says she can't trust me. She doesn't want to get married yet. She likes men, she even flirts with my old man—you've seen her." Crow smiles to show that he's okay with this, but his face has a tight savage look as it had when he was fighting with T-Man. "Anyway, I'm going. Claudette can be a bitch, but she agrees a boy needs his father."

All this while I've been standing a few feet from Crow, staring at him, unmoving. My eyes are blinded with tears. I want to protest, *You are so much a better person than Claudette! You are the most wonderful person I know.*

I want to protest how wrong this is. Crow is leaving Yarrow Lake, I will never see him again.

Crow says, teasing, "Now you can cross the bridge, Jenna, What's to cry about?"

"I don't want you to go away, Gabriel. Please."

Crow, about to buckle the strap of the crash helmet beneath his chin, thinks better of what he's doing and lowers the helmet onto my head. "For you, *chérie*. In case." The helmet must look comical on me, it's so big. The sides come down past my chin. Crow laughs at me, I'm so dazed. He frames my face in his hands. For a moment I think that he will shut my eyes with his thumbs as he did back at the creek but instead he leans down to kiss me.

A warm kiss, on my mouth. A kiss light as a feather.

"I'll always be your friend, *chérie*. You know that."

But Crow, I want to protest, I love you.

Instead I say, in the calmest voice I can manage, "I will always be your friend too, Gabriel. Forever."

24

I guess I want to live, Mom.
   I want to live forever!

25

Jenna! Jen-na!

Mid race I hear her. Pounding the dirt track, I hear her. In the final stretch of the half-mile sprint I hear her.

Jen-na! In the rush of blood in my ears I hear her, a voice distinct among the others uplifted and aroused.

The lead runner flies across the finish line, in her bronze gold T-shirt and shorts—Yarrow High. Second runner flies across the finish line, dark crimson for Canaan High. Third runner, one of ours. And fourth: me.

Out of a field of ten. Fourth place!

Sweaty, panting like a dog. I'm limping and my hair is in my face and I was really losing it in the final stretch, but anyway, I am *so happy*.

My teammates are hugging one another. Hugging me. Dara Bowen is hugging me. Yarrow High has won the half-mile sprint. We're giddy, laughing. We're exhausted but triumphant.

The next race, a mile sprint, other teammates are racing, maybe they won't win. Maybe we won't win the meet with Canaan High. But we've won the half-mile sprint, we're jubilant.

Aunt Caroline comes to hug me. Not minding my sweaty T-shirt. "Jenna, you were wonderful! What did I tell you?" My little cousins Becky and Mikey are congratulating me too.

So I'm not the slowest runner on the Yarrow High girls' track team.

I will never be the fastest, but who cares?

Mom didn't. Aunt Caroline doesn't.

The team captain, who's a new friend of mine, gives me a wink. "Hey, J-J, somebody's got to come in fourth."

J-J is, like, my new name here. Why, I don't know.

We're all so sweaty it's gross. We need to shower and change our clothes. I'm still panting. Could've come in fifth, could've come in tenth. Could've collapsed at the halfway point—my knee is giving me pain. This didn't happen! I am *so happy*.

It's a warm May afternoon. I am sixteen years old. It's almost a year since the wreck. I can see the white Honda moving onto the bridge that's so vast, it seems to open out into nothingness—into the blue. In the sky, snow geese are flying in V formation.

In the sky here, geese are flying overhead too. It's these geese I have been hearing. Not snow geese but Canada geese. As they beat their wings, they emit strange honking cries that sound like human voices, fading. Why? I wonder. I wish I'd asked Crow, Crow might've known.

Crow said the geese migrate north to a colder climate. It's a sign of spring.

After the meet, Christa Shaw has invited us to her house, which is close by, to celebrate. Maybe, I tell her. Maybe I'll come join you, in a little while.

Joyce Carol Oates is the renowned author of many novels. Her first novel for teens, *Big Mouth & Ugly Girl*, was a finalist for the *Los Angeles Times* Book Prize, followed by *Freaky Green Eyes*, a *Publishers Weekly* Best Book, and *Sexy*. In 2003 she was a recipient of the Common Wealth Award for Distinguished Service in Literature. A recipient of the National Book Award and the PEN/Malamud Award for Excellence in Short Fiction, Ms. Oates is the Roger S. Berlind Distinguished Professor of the Humanities at Princeton University. She lives in Princeton, New Jersey.